RUDOLPH THE RED-NOSED BUMPKIN

SAM CHEEVER

ELECTRIC PROSE PUBLICATIONS

* * *

Rudolph the Red-Nosed Bumpkin, died a very shiny death...

Rudy-Bob Hortmann has never quite gotten the hang of making friends. He doesn't much like peopling, mostly preferring the company of his pot-bellied pig, Ethel Squeaks to humanoid types. But there's one exception. Rudy-Bob loves kids. So for Christmas every year he gives himself a present. He plays Santa at the annual Deer Hollow Christmas party. Only this year, Rudy-Bob doesn't make it out of the Santa suit when the Pageant is done. Instead, Deputy Sheriff Arno Willager finds Rudy-Bob literally chillin' in a snowbank, his bulbous nose flashing red through the snow.

That's where I come into the picture. I'm Joey Fulle, and I'm pretty good at finding bodies around my place on the outskirts of Deer Hollow. I didn't actually find this one, of course. But I'm fully invested in locating his killer. 'Cause, with the help of my handsome PI boyfriend Hal, my sweet and goofy Pitbull Caphy, and my opinionated Siamese cat, LaLee, I'm also pretty good at finding killers. Sometimes, even before they find me…

STAY IN TOUCH

I don't give away a lot of books. But I value my readers and, to show it, I'm gifting you a copy of a novella from my fun Silver Hills Mystery series just for signing up for my newsletter!

SIGN UP HERE!

CHAPTER 1

Imagine my surprise when I walked into my house after the Christmas party at Deer Hollow Town Hall and found my blonde, green-eyed Pitbull, Caphy frothing at the mouth with bright green frosting, and my sophisticated and elegant Siamese cat, LaLee draped glassy-eyed over a branch of the Christmas tree, a pink yarn ball cuddled in her arms like a precious bundle of joy.

I looked from one to the other, unsure what to address first. Behind me, I could feel shock radiating off Hal and knew without looking that he was gawking at the cat.

Never in my wildest dreams would I have ever suspected LaLee had it in her to be goofy. But then I'd never gotten her a catnip ball before.

I grimaced at the sight of her long limbs hanging limply over the branch and scanned a horrified look at the broken ornaments on the floor beneath her. "Oh no!" I hurried over, picking up the adorable Pitbull ornament my friend Lis had bought me the first Christmas Caphy and I had shared together.

I frowned at the cat, whose lids drooped as if she'd been drinking whiskey-spiked eggnog all day. "Bad, kitty!"

LaLee purred even louder, trying to roll over on the wimpy branch and wrapping her long legs even tighter around the ball.

Hal took the broken ornament from me. His handsome face folded into a frown as he examined it, his dark green gaze sliding to mine. "I think I can glue it back together."

I nodded. "Look at this fool cat. She's huggin' that catnip ornament like a drunk hugs a bottle of hooch."

Hal gave me a one-armed hug. "Maybe we should put it into a paper bag for her."

"Har," I said, grinning. "Stupid cat." I reached to pluck her out of the tree, but as soon as I tried to lift her free, her gaze sharpened and she yowled, swiping me with a claw and drawing blood down my arm in a long scratch.

I jerked my arm back. "Ouch!"

LaLee's sudden movement over-balanced her and she slipped off the branch. She scrabbled for purchase, her claws shredding a couple of my silk-covered bulbs and dragging the string of old-fashioned boiling candlesticks down with her.

Her catnip ball stuck in the tree as she fell.

LaLee hit the wrapped presents beneath the tree and immediately sprang up with another yowl, trying to leap back up to reclaim her catnip ball.

Unfortunately for her, I was faster.

I ripped the ornament off the branch and held it above my head as she leaped, slashing at the air beneath the prize.

It was only a matter of time before those claws connected with flesh. I panicked, looking at Hal. "Here!" I threw it at him and his dark green gaze went wide as he caught it, bobbled it a few times in his panic, and then made a small sound of alarm as the cat turned her attention to him.

"Oh no," he murmured, starting to backtrack as the catnip-crazed cat stalked in his direction, a growl vibrating her narrow chest.

"Run!" I told Hal and giggled as he took off like a shot, LaLee five feet behind him and gaining fast.

Hal leaped off the floor and hit the couch, his stocking feet hitting the cushion and leaping the back, only to find himself looking into the cat's feral gaze when he landed.

She'd leaped from the floor onto the back of the couch, foregoing the first step that would have slowed her down.

Caphy stood in the entryway, tail enthusiastically

wagging as she watched the show. Hal jerked his arm away with a shout, barely avoiding a swipe of the razor-sharp claws, and Caphy barked gleefully, her nails making a happy clicking sound on the tile.

"Get the door," Hal yelled, jumping sideways and leaping the coffee table to dodge around the outside of the room and run for the front door.

With a shriek, I took off running, Hal with his dangerous baggage held high barreling in my direction.

I managed to wrench the door open just as he skidded across the tiles, and Hal threw the offending yarn ball through the open door, into the night.

LaLee might have been under the influence, but she wasn't stupid. She hated snow and cold with the heat of a thousand suns. She threw on the brakes three feet from the door and skidded all the way to the threshold, a disappointed yowl wafting out into the snowy night and dying under the weight of the Winter storm.

With a delighted bark, Caphy shot past her, nearly blowing her off her drugged feet, and bounced out into the snow to retrieve the ball.

I quickly shut the door behind her. I figured it would take her all of about thirty seconds to shred the stupid ball out there.

I'd retrieve the bits and pieces in the Spring.

Hal held his hand up and I slapped my palm against it.

"Note to self, my cat is a catnip addict. Never buy her catnip toys."

There was a scratch on the front door. I opened it and Caphy trotted in looking proud and happy, pink yarn hanging from her face to mingle with the frosting. She stopped inside the door and shook herself, throwing snow all over Hal and me and my poor tile.

I sighed. "I guess we might as well go see the damage in the kitchen."

"I'll get some paper towels for this floor," Hal said.

I nodded, tucking a long strand of red-blonde hair behind my ear. "I'm afraid to see how many cookies she ate." I'd been a baking maniac for days, baking cookies to gift all my friends and a few dozen for the town Christmas party we'd attended that night. As usual, the party had really put me into the holiday spirit, filled with food, friends, sugar and all my favorite Christmas songs.

I'd enjoyed watching all the kids climb up on Santa's lap, not one of them suspecting who really lived beneath the hat and beard. If they had, they would have asked where Ethel Squeaks, his beloved pot-bellied pig was.

Rudy Hortmann would have no doubt loved to bring his pig to the party, but having her there would have given him away. Everybody in Deer Hollow knew how much Rudy loved that pig. Even the kids would have seen beyond the beard and red velvet suit if he'd had Ethel Squeaks sitting next to him on the dais.

We entered the kitchen to find colorful cardboard strewn across the floor, the remains of the tissue paper I'd cushioned the baked goodies with providing colorful confetti among the ripped and shredded cookie box corpse.

What we didn't find was a single cookie crumb. My naughty pibl hadn't allowed a single grain of sugar to escape her ravenous appetite.

"Well, it looks like she only got hold of Lis's box," Hal said, quickly taking stock of the carefully compiled boxes on the counter.

Caphy wilted under my steely blue glare, her guilt a finely-honed thing that she'd had years of misbehavior to perfect. Unfortunately for me and my cookies, guilt wasn't enough to keep her from misbehaving in the first place.

Lucky for my sweet pibl, she was much too cute for me to stay mad. And, glancing toward my bleeding arm, at least she was smart enough to look guilty. Unlike the snotty feline I could see bathing on the windowsill as if she'd never done violence against me and embarrassed herself hanging in the tree like a drunk.

"You need to put something on that scratch," Hal told me, taking my arm and examining it carefully.

"It's not very deep. I'm fine."

He shook his dark head, kissing me on the nose. "Cat's claws are full of germs. If you don't clean and put something on that, it's going to get infected."

Sighing, I took a look at the mess on the floor.

"This will wait a couple of minutes," Hal assured me. "Caphy and I will get started on it while you're gone."

He wasn't joking about that. My adorable pibl was happily ripping a piece of white tissue paper into pieces and eating it.

I sighed. "Don't let her eat too much of that paper. She's going to be horking it up all night."

He nodded, grinning. "If she's up horking all night it will more than likely be from the dozen Christmas cookies she ate than from that paper."

"Or the catnip and string," I mused, shaking my head. "It's a wonder she's survived as long as she has. That dog will eat anything."

I heard Hal's phone ring as I headed upstairs. I quickly dressed the wound and took a moment to change into comfy clothes and brush my hair before heading back down to the kitchen.

LaLee met me on the bottom stair and rubbed against my ankles, purring as if she hadn't tried to eat me in favor of her drug of choice.

"Yeah, nice try, girlfriend. I'm gonna need a minute to forgive you for slicing my arm open and your general killer attitude."

Hal had a half-full trash bag in one hand and his

cell phone in the other. He looked up as I came into the room. "Yeah, I'm at Joey's. Should we meet you there?"

He listened for a beat and then nodded. "We'll be there in five minutes."

"What's up?" I asked, not thrilled at the idea of going back out into the winter wonderland. I'd been looking forward to making some hot chocolate with tiny marshmallows and cuddling on the couch to watch the snow come down beyond the windows.

Hal frowned. "I'm afraid it's bad news. Arno found a body in the snow not too far from here."

CHAPTER 2

The wind had temporarily died down, leaving behind a soft flutter of large snowflakes that obscured the night sky and slowly but steadily covered everything it touched in a blanket of pristine white.

The air smelled crisp and clean. The silent fall of the snow was magical. And the thickly covered branches of the surrounding evergreens were like something from a Hallmark Christmas movie.

Unfortunately, the bright lights blinking through their gentle blanket of snow a few feet away did not belong in the same movie.

As I stood quivering in my boots, hands jammed deep inside the pockets of my puffy winter coat to keep my fingers from succumbing to frostbite even covered in fur-lined leather gloves, I couldn't help the feeling of sad expectation that overcame me as

Deputy Arno Willager dropped to one knee beside the blinking lights and carefully scraped aside the obscuring layer of snow. The still-flickering light played over his thick mop of blonde hair, sparkling on the snow that had fallen there.

I sucked in a horrified breath. The wide brown eyes stared unseeing toward the falling curtain of white. The mouth was open, the tongue swollen and exposed, and a pretty strand of Christmas lights entwined the purple flesh above his fake-fur-lined collar.

Rudy-Bob, a.k.a. Rudolph Robert Hortmann, had been strangled with a strand of lights that I presumed belonged to the nearest evergreen, since the strand was partially tangled on one of its wide, lower branches and a thick, bright orange extension cord led from the underside of the same tree, toward the small, pale-wood cabin in the near distance.

"Is that Rudy's house?" Hal asked, his voice muted by the icy wind and obscuring snow.

Arno stood, his brown gaze sliding away from Rudy, toward the little cabin. He nodded. A shrill screeching filled the air, seeming to come from Rudy's home. Arno sighed. "I'm guessing by that racket that Ethel Squeaks saw the whole thing."

Hal looked up from the corpse. "Ethel? Was Rudy-Bob in a relationship?"

Arno's answering smile was grim. "It's his pot-bellied pig. The two of them are inseparable."

A terrible, sad feeling slid through me. "Poor thing." Tears filled my gaze at the desperate-sounding squeals and snorts coming from the cabin. "Who will take her now?"

Arno pulled a pair of heavy gloves from his coat pockets, jamming them on his already red hands. "Rudy didn't have any family that I know of."

"She's not going to the pound," I told my friend, catching his glare and seeing the resignation in his brown eyes. "Joey…"

I shook my head. "I'll keep her until we can find her a home. I'm not letting that poor creature go into that place. It will kill her to lose him and then find herself in a cage."

"They do the best they can at the pound, Joey," Hal said, reprimanding me.

I realized how I'd sounded and grimaced. "I didn't mean the people at the pound don't try to be kind. I know they do. But this animal has already lost the person she loved most in the world. Being shoved into that environment would break her heart."

"You sound as if you know her," Arno said, glaring at me.

I crossed my arms, shivering as the wind kicked back up, sending snow drifting from the evergreens to join the thickening curtain of the stuff falling from the sky. "I don't need to *know* her Arno." My voice caught as tears slipped from my eyes. "I only need to *hear* her."

A fresh squeal of pure pain cut through the snow and wind as if to prove my point.

Arno sighed. "Well, you don't need to worry. My mom had a pot-bellied pig when she was a kid. She'll help us find the right home for Ethel Squeaks."

My lungs unclenched and I took a deep, quivering breath, nodding. "Thanks, Arno."

Hal wrapped an arm around my shoulders and pulled me close, kissing my temple.

I sniffed, in a less than ladylike way and felt my heart tighten with grief as my gaze fell on Rudy again. "He was such a sweet man. Awkward. But sweet. He loved playing Santa."

"The kids really liked him too," Hal offered. "He took extra time with each of them."

Arno looked thoughtful. "He did seem a bit subdued tonight, though."

I shook my head. "I hadn't noticed." I felt guilty for not noticing.

Arno stood another moment, thoughtful, and then he looked up. His expression was cool, clinical, cop-like. "It's going to be nearly impossible to gather any evidence out here. Between the snow and the wind, there won't be much to find. But I need to figure out a way to solve this, and I'm going to need your help."

He was addressing Hal, whose background as a cop and then a private investigator made him an apt deputy when Hal was short-handed. He might be disappointed when he found out I was going to help too. Hal and I were a package deal. I claimed the right to tag along based on the fact that nobody in Deer Hollow had found as many corpses over the last year as I had.

Including Arno.

"I'm guessing you're short-staffed because of the holidays," I said. "Since you're asking for our help."

Arno opened his mouth, probably to argue that he hadn't asked for *my* help, but seemed to change his mind. He might be disappointed to know that I was going to tag along, but I was pretty sure he wasn't surprised. I'd been a thorn in his side during every murder investigation since I'd found my first corpse in a wood chipper on my property.

"I'm the only one who doesn't have a family," he said a bit bleakly. "So, I'm on call pretty much twenty-four-seven until after Christmas."

I patted him on the arm. "You're a good man, Charlie Brown."

His laugh was abrupt, humorless. "Like I'm going to believe anything *you* tell me, Lucy."

Sirens burst through the clogging moisture in the air and throbbed toward us. Glancing in the direction of Deer Hollow, I could see the flashing glow of them burning through the night.

Arno looked at Hal. "Help me search the body and get pictures?"

Hal nodded, and the two of them crouched down beside poor Rudy.

I turned away, unwilling to watch as the sweet man I'd offered cookies and apple cider to earlier that night officially became a murder investigation.

I wandered over to the tree where the strand of lights had been wrapped, wondering if Rudy had noticed the lights were askew when he'd approached his house.

Maybe Ethel had warned him someone was in the yard. If she had, would he have listened? Would a bunch of extra squealing sink in? Or would he have written it off as excitement in seeing him?

Illuminating the spot with a small but powerful flashlight, I leaned over and carefully peered underneath the tree. Protected by the upper branches, the snow was much thinner in the dirt beneath the tree. It didn't appear churned up as if someone had moved around under there, but with the ground so frozen, I wasn't sure it would have anyway.

I took a few steps away so I wouldn't track up any evidence, and walked around the tree, examining the snow in a futile search for prints. Any shoeprints the killer might have made would have long since been obscured by wind and snow. I lifted my head and examined the ground between where I stood and the road. If someone had walked from Goose Down Road, they would have had to park on the snow-covered shoulder. The weight of a vehicle would have packed the snow deeper and harder. That kind of track would be more difficult to hide.

I started off in that direction, hunching against the icy wind. While it had died down closer to Rudy's cabin, which was surrounded by trees and had been built in a bit of a low spot in the hilly landscape, it was still brutal and blustery in the flat, open land between the house and the road.

I ducked into a small copse of trees a few yards from Goose Down Road to shake off the brutal assault for a beat. The cluster of trunks and drooping branches of the old-growth evergreens were like a haven in the midst of the violent bluster.

I realized the killer might have waited there for Rudy to return home. Or he might have sheltered in the spot for a minute as I was doing, just to get out of the weather. The thought had me looking around on the pine-needle strewn dirt for any evidence that someone had recently stood underneath the trees.

I found a single, shallow footprint a few feet from where I stood. It looked too big to be mine, but I quickly checked the tread against my furry boots to be sure. Then I lifted my gaze to the prickly branches, looking for a strand of hair or a sliver of cloth that might tell me more.

I found nothing, though it was dark enough it

didn't surprise me I hadn't. We definitely needed to revisit the spot in daylight.

Hal called my name, his voice tinged with worry. I stepped out and waved. I didn't bother to yell at the men about my discovery, the wind would make it nearly impossible for them to hear.

Hal waved back and returned to his work near the body. I stepped out of the copse and headed for the road.

Two cars were parked across Goose Down Road, blocking it from through traffic. Arno's lights were flashing a warning through the snowy dark, and Hal had left his emergency lights flashing on his big SUV.

Arno had set flares a quarter mile up in either direction to keep any cars coming up on us from crashing into the barricade.

Looking at the thick gloss on the surface of Goose Down Road, I doubted anybody would be driving fast enough to consider it a crash.

Maybe a bump.

Rudy's old pickup truck was pulled just off the road, the front tires stuck in the deep snow of what I assumed was his driveway. The back just barely cleared the road. He would have walked from the truck down his long drive toward the house. He'd probably been hunched into his coat, head down, and his hearing would have been hampered by the wind.

He'd have been a sitting duck for the killer.

Pain rolled over in my chest and kicked against my ribs. My eyes burned with tears I blinked away for fear they'd freeze to ice on my cheeks.

I walked a distance along the shoulder and saw nothing that would indicate another car had been parked there. Eyeing Hal's SUV with longing, I burrowed more deeply into my coat and forced myself to retrace my steps and walk the other way from Rudy's drive. I found the spot about thirty yards up.

Black oil stained the packed snow, and skid marks marked the spot where a vehicle with nearly bald tires fought for purchase on the shoulder.

I turned at the sound of footsteps crunching toward me, finding Hal, his fine Greek nose bright red from the cold, looking miserable as he approached. I pointed to the marks in the snow and the oil. "This might be the killer's tracks."

He crouched down and ran his fingers along the skid marks. "Either an older vehicle…" he nodded toward the oil stain. "Or one that hasn't been well cared for."

An icy breeze bit against the back of my neck, and I shivered so violently my teeth clacked together.

Hal straightened up and wrapped an arm around me, pressing cool lips to my temple. "Arno wants us to fetch the pig. He's got to stay with the body."

Two radio cars from the Sheriff's office rolled up on the scene, lights flashing. They'd shut the sirens off as they hit Goose Down Road, probably not wanting to scare the locals.

A tiny man dressed in Sheriff's browns climbed out and lifted his hand to us. "Evenin' Joey, Hal."

We waved back. "Hey, Deputy Sheppard!" I called out.

Deputy Mark Sheppard might be the tiniest cop on the job. He stood eye to eye with me, and I was only five foot four. Also, I was pretty sure my arms were bigger around than his legs. Sheppard made me feel huge.

We'd worked with the deputy on our last case, when somebody had killed a neighbor of Arno's mom's and most of Deer Hollow were suspects. He'd been annoying, a little dense about interpersonal cues, and pretty full of himself. But in the end, he'd proven to be a decent cop.

Hal and I headed down Rudy's snow-covered driveway, the snow coming almost to my knees in spots. I was panting by the time we reached the cabin, but at least I felt a bit warmer from the effort.

An ambulance had arrived by the time Hal picked the front lock and two men, carrying a stretcher between them, were making their way toward Arno and Rudy.

Hal shoved the front door open and motioned for me to go on inside. A brittle blast of wind , snow against my back and neck and all but blew me into the cozy little cabin. I stopped on a colorful rag rug in front of the door and looked around, seeing the warm glow of embers flaring in the stone fireplace as the outside air fed the dying flame.

Hal pushed the front door closed and gave a violent shiver, stomping his boots on the rug and tugging off his wet coat. He hung it on a hook behind the door and I gave him mine, sliding off my ice-laden boots and leaving them on the rug.

I glanced quickly around the room, noting the overstuffed couch and recliner positioned to take best advantage of the fireplace. A large, flat-screen TV was hung over the mantel. A child's teepee sat in the corner nearest the fire, a pink fleece blanket trailing out of it onto the bright rag rug.

A soft snuffling sound brought my attention around and, a small black and white pig came trotting out to investigate us.

The friendly little pet ran over and snorfled my feet, its curly tail spinning happily. I bent down and scratched the little pig between its enormous ears. "Hello, Ethel Squeaks. How are you?"

The pig ran toward the fireplace and found a big, bright yellow ball, shoving it with her snout and then running after it as I smiled.

Hal came up beside me. "Pigs play with balls? Crazy."

"I know, right?" Watching Ethel play, my heart

twisted painfully. Though she seemed happy to have company, she kept casting her gaze toward the front door, no doubt anxious to see her favorite human again.

I sat down on the floor in front of the fire and Ethel draped herself along the floor beside me, sighing happily. "I want a pig," I told Hal.

He rolled his eyes. "There's a big surprise."

I sniffled and he caught my eye. "I was just teasing, honey."

Shaking my head, I ran the back of my hand under my leaking eyes. "It's not that. I'm just feeling sad for Ethel. She keeps looking for Rudy."

Hal frowned, nodding. "We'll find her somebody to love, Joey. You have my word on that."

I sniffed again. "I know."

The door opened and Arno came inside, stomping his boots and shoving the door closed with a grunt. "It's painful out there."

Ethel trotted over and stopped, staring at him through her small eyes, big ears flipping and tail twitching uncertainly.

Arno narrowed his gaze. "Is it going to eat me?"

"Not without a good Hollandaise," Hal said, grinning.

"Har," Arno said. He slowly bent down and offered Ethel the back of his hand, like he would a strange dog.

The pig hesitated, her big head tipping upward to

stare at him. Her snout twitched. Apparently deciding he was harmless, Ethel Squeaks ran over and sniffed his boots before dropping right onto them with a soft groan.

Arno glanced at us, perplexed. "Um. It's …er…on my feet."

Hal looked around. "I guess we should give the place a quick look to see if there's anything here that would point to a possible motive."

Hal headed toward the back of the cabin.

I moved into the kitchen.

As I searched the drawers of a small, antique rolltop desk Rudy had clearly refinished, the sound of a clearing throat came from the living room. "Um, Joey…"

I grinned, ignoring the cop. It was too much fun seeing him discombobulated to rescue him right away.

The drawers held a small baggie filled with coins, a leash and collar which Rudy probably used to take Ethel for walks, some candles, and a couple of small flashlights.

I checked under the rolltop and found a notepaper pad bearing a picture of a man and a pig on the top. Across the bottom was printed, "From the nest of Ethel Squeaks and Rudy-Bob Hortmann."

Heaviness settled on my chest. The uncommon pair had clearly been a family. As far as I knew, Rudy had no other family. He'd clearly loved the pig very much.

"Joey?" Arno's voice had achieved a slightly hysterical edge.

Sighing, I stuck my head through the door. "What is it, Arno?"

Ethel had rolled over, still draped across his shoes, and was showing him her belly.

"What do I do now?"

"Obviously, you're not a farm boy," I said, teasing him.

He glowered over at me. "I know dogs and a little bit about cats, but pigs are a whole different universe for me."

I took pity on him. "She's very sweet. She just wants you to rub her belly."

I returned to the kitchen, tugging cabinets open and searching through plastic ware, a random assortment of chipped and aged dishes, and what appeared to be every cleaning agent known to man beneath the farmhouse sink.

I didn't have a clue what I was looking for. But whatever it was, I probably didn't find it. The closest I came to discovering anything at all controversial was the bottle of medicine tucked into the front corner of Rudy's spice cabinet. I pulled it out and set it on the counter.

The pantry was full to bursting with boxes and cans of food. Rudy had enough food to hunker down and ride out the current snowstorm. Unfortunately, he wouldn't be there to eat it.

The floor beneath the shelves of food held a food processor, a blender, and a crockpot. Tucked behind the rarely used kitchen tools was a metal container decorated in Christmas colors. I pulled it out and wrenched the lid off, noting the scratched and dulled Santa Clause and Rudolf depicted on its front. The tin was clearly an old one, the dented surface telling me it had suffered a lot of use.

Tattered white tissue paper filled the tin to the brim. I frowned, realizing it was too heavy to be just tissue paper. The paper clearly hid something bigger.

I was only mildly surprised when I tugged the paper aside and saw the gun. I carried the box to the counter and set it next to the bottle of pills. "Arno. I need you to come here, please."

"What's wrong?" he asked a moment later when he entered the kitchen, a miniature pot-bellied pig trotting at his heels.

I pointed to my collection of finds. He frowned when he saw the gun. "Where was this?"

"Hidden behind some stuff in the pantry."

He nodded, Arno picked up the bottle of pills. I noticed he was wearing latex gloves and sighed. I hadn't thought to ask for some. It looked like he'd be using the prints he'd taken from me a few weeks ago to eliminate my prints from evidence. "Clozaril," he said. "This is an antipsychotic medication."

Hal came into the room. "Antipsychotic? As in for schizophrenia?"

Arno glanced at him. "Or bipolar disease," he agreed. "I had no idea Rudy was struggling with anything like that."

"Me neither," I agreed. "Though I didn't know him well. I've mostly only spent time with him at the annual Christmas party."

Arno jerked his head toward the gun. "Not a good combination with that," he said, frowning.

"No, it isn't," Hal agreed. "And it seems unlikely he could have purchased the gun with a diagnosis of psychosis."

"Thirty-eight special," Arno said, snapping the chamber open and looking inside. "Two bullets in the cylinder." He snapped it closed again, settling it back into the box. "I'll have this tested and check to see if it belonged to Rudy." He dropped the pill bottle into a small paper envelope and wrote the location on the outside. "I'll also call the doctor on this bottle and see what our victim was suffering from."

Hal and I looked down as Ethel grunted loudly. She sniffed the box and seemed to become agitated, squealing, and rocking on her hooves.

Arno headed for the door with his evidence. "Can you two find a carrier or something for the pig? I'll take her to the pound before I turn this in."

"Stop right there, Arno," I said.

Arno stopped in the kitchen doorway and sighed,

turning slowly to me. "Joey we're not going to keep going through this…"

"I told you, this animal is not going to the pound."

He looked down at his feet, seeming to struggle for patience. When he looked up again, he looked resigned. He and I had danced this dance before. "What do you suggest?"

I shook my head. "I have no idea. I only know we can't put her into a cage."

Arno and I stared at each other, his stubborn battling my stubborn across the space between us. Finally, Hal broke the impasse. "I'll take her to my house until we can figure out where she's going."

I grinned, giving him a hug.

Arno just shook his head. "You two deserve each other."

CHAPTER 3

I was sitting on the floor in front of Hal's fire, leaning against the couch and feeding Ethel bites of pizza when Arno called the next day. I knew I shouldn't do it. All the information we'd found online said not to overfeed the pig. But when I'd discovered she could lift one hoof to beg, I was lost.

Hal arched a midnight brow at me as he answered his phone. "Hey, Arno."

I gave Ethel the bite, and she immediately lifted her tiny hoof again. "No," I told my adorable sidekick. "I just got the look from the Greek god. You're cut off." I scratched between her oversized ears, grinning as her tiny eyes closed with pleasure.

"Yeah, the pig's fine. But we're going to need to put her belly on one of those rolling things by the time Joey gets done with her."

I stuck my tongue out at him, settling back against the couch and adjusting the fleece covering my legs. The fire crackled warmly, and I smiled as Ethel Squeaks dove into the blanket and made a nest before flopping onto her side in front of the fire.

"No kidding?" Hal said, dropping onto the couch. His muscular thigh bumped gently against my shoulder and I leaned into it, enjoying his heat. "Wait, let me put you on speaker so Joey can hear." He hit the speaker button. "Okay, Arno, can you say that again?"

"Hey, Joey."

"Hey," I responded, moving my legs so Ethel had more room to snuggle into the blanket.

"The gun you found came back as one that was used in a crime in Bloomington, Indiana two years ago."

I sat forward, "Are you serious?"

"As serious as the heart attack you're going to give that pig if you keep overfeeding her."

"Ha!" I said. "Was Rudy implicated in the crime?"

"No. The gun's not registered to him. It actually belonged to an elderly man in Indianapolis. He reported it stolen a few years ago."

"This investigation is covering some ground," Hal said. "Have you spoken to the Indy cops? Do they believe it was stolen?"

"I have, and they do. The owner was in his nineties at the time. According to his daughter he put it on a garage sale table, not thinking about it, and it disappeared."

"Awesome," Hal said, shaking his head. "Some creep probably couldn't believe his luck."

"Yeah. It was used a few months later to kill a young woman at Indiana University. The Bloomington police never caught the guy who killed her."

"Guy? Did they have a description?" Hal asked.

"A vague one. Thirties, white guy, messy brown hair, and filthy clothes. They actually questioned a local homeless guy a few times, but they couldn't make anything stick."

"Is the homeless guy still around?" I asked.

"Not sure. I'm going to drive down there this afternoon. Would you guys like to tag along?"

Hal looked at me and I nodded. "Sure," he said.

Then I remembered I had to take LaLee to the vet. "Oh. I can't. I have an appointment."

"Hal, I'll pick you up in about an hour."

Hal disconnected and gave me an assessing look.

"What?" I asked him.

"You really have an appointment? This isn't about what happened *here*?"

I had to think about what he was asking me for a beat before it fell into place. Hal and I had met over the murder of a homeless guy. He was wondering if I was afraid speaking with another homeless man would trigger something dark I'd rather not remember. "No. I really do have an appointment. LaLee has a bleeding tooth that I need to get checked. Doc Beetle had to squeeze us in today. If I don't take her today I won't be able to get it looked at for a week."

"A week? Has there been a run on checkups?"

"Canine flu epidemic, actually. Doc's been working twelve-hour days, I guess. He sounded exhausted when I spoke to him." Given that Deer Hollow's only veterinarian was older than the sands of time, it wasn't healthy for him to work himself so hard.

"He's going to have to bite the bullet and hire a partner," Hal said, shaking his head.

I laughed. "I'll let you tell him that. He's even more stubborn than a mule. It would be an insult to mules to compare him to them."

Hal slipped down to the floor and wrapped an arm around my shoulders. We sat in companionable silence for several moments, enjoying the crackle of the fire and the snoring of the pig.

Watching Ethel sleep, I realized I was grinning again. "She's a remarkable animal," I told Hal.

He nodded. "Smart as a whip. I'm really glad Rudy litter box trained her though. I'd hate to have to take her outside in this weather."

I nodded agreement. I was happy Caphy took herself out and seemed to mostly enjoy playing in the snow after she did her business. But I had noticed that, since the winter storm showed up, she didn't stay outside all that long. "Good thing LaLee uses a box. There's no way I'd get that stubborn critter outside right now."

Silence fell between us again. Watching Ethel, I couldn't help believing that Rudy had been a good man. He'd loved his pet unconditionally. He'd been so good to the kids every Christmas. There were no signs that he could be a killer.

"Do you really think Rudy killed that woman?" I asked Hal.

He shrugged. "We never know what people are capable of. But I'm determined to find out. For all the good Rudy did here in Deer Hollow, we owe him that."

I nodded. As usual, my PI had put voice to my exact thought.

* * *

*D*oc Beetle's assistant, Sally Moore wasn't sitting at her desk when we came through the door. I moved away from the door and the residual cold air hovering there and placed LaLee's carrier down as I took a seat.

A plaintive yowl emerged from under the blanket I'd draped over the carrier to keep the cat warm. "You think it's bad in there," I muttered to my cat. "You should be out here."

Her yowl gained steam and attitude, the Siamese cat being her usual mouthy, opinionated self.

From somewhere in the back of the clinic, a mournful howl filled the air, the sad singer immediately picking up another stanza of his or her song as soon as the previous notes ran down.

Quick footsteps sounded beyond the door into the exam rooms. A beat later, Sally bustled through, her cheeks rosy and her uniform looking rumpled. The usually tidy and calm veterinary assistant looked a bit harried. Her dark blonde hair was messy as if she'd been continually running her fingers through it, and an assortment of stains splotched the cat and dog covered scrubs she wore.

"Oh, Joey!" The petite, middle-aged woman gave me a weary smile, her hazel gaze friendly despite the appearance of being rushed. "I'm so sorry. I didn't hear the bell with all the caterwauling going on back there." She laughed good-naturedly. "Thor doesn't like being away from home, I'm afraid."

I grinned. "Husky?"

Sally nodded. "Sweet dog. He's just getting over the flu." She frowned. "Nasty strain. He's young and strong and nearly didn't make it."

No wonder Sally looked harried. "Caphy's due for shots soon, should I risk bringing her in?"

"Probably not. It's better for her to be a bit past due than to be exposed to this. We're asking all clients to keep visits to the clinic to a minimum until we get this under control."

I nodded, glancing down at the carrier. Growling, snorfling sounds had replaced the plaintive yowling of before. "Is LaLee safe?"

Sally hesitated. "The strain we've been seeing here is not indicated to be a danger to cats. Cats have shown susceptibility to the newer strains, though. The risk is low. But if you don't feel comfortable having us see her..."

I really considered taking her back home, but I was starting to worry about her behavior. "If the risk is low, I'll chance it. She hasn't been eating well lately, and her face looks swollen. I found some blood on the floor near her bowl yesterday. I'm worried about her."

Sally nodded. "I'll tell Doc you're here. We're using the mourning room for non-infective patients right now so you should be extra safe with her. Come on back, and we'll get you situated."

The mourning room was set up with two small couches and a soft rug on the floor. Beautiful framed poems about pet loss adorned the walls, and the lighting was low until Sally hit a switch near the door, plunging us into patient-room-level brightness.

She tugged a rolling table away from the wall and spritzed it with rubbing alcohol, giving it a careful going over with paper towels. "I'll just get her stats and then Doc will have a look at that mouth."

I uncovered the carrier and let LaLee stroll out on

her own. I'd learned early in our relationship never to stick my hand into LaLee's kennel. She had a full set of claws and knew how to use them. If the claws failed to subdue her victim, the Siamese cat was not averse to using her needle-like teeth to drive the point home.

When I picked her up, she hissed, but as soon as I settled her onto the table, LaLee started purring, rubbing against Sally as the vet assistant gave her a quick once-over.

"Such a pretty girl," Sally crooned, captivated by the rarely-seen-in-captivity LaLee charm. "And so sweet."

I snorted, earning myself a glare from the cat. "Don't be fooled, I'm pretty sure she recently came through a portal from Hell."

LaLee yowled in my direction and then went back to sucking up to Sally.

"Beware the demon under the pretty fur, though," I warned Sally. "When you stick that thing in her butt, you might be getting a full-on demonic experience."

Sally giggled. "You're so funny, Joey."

Moments later, Sally staggered from the room, nursing a fresh scratch along her forearm and making the sign of the cross over her chest.

I glared at my non-repentant cat. "That was *not* a nice girl," I told her.

She gave me a soft growl and rolled over onto

her back. I tried to resist scratching the cute, furry offering but failed.

I was still scratching her belly when Doc Beetle bustled through the door. "Afternoon, Joey."

"Hey, Doc."

He washed his hands while perusing the notes Sally had made on LaLee's chart. "Sounds like our girl's got a problem with her mouth."

I nodded. "I'm hoping it's just a tooth."

He dried his hands on a paper towel. "Let's just have a look and see." The elderly vet walked over and stood beside the table, giving LaLee his best quelling look. "Here's how it's going to go down, Miss LaLee. I'm going to look at your mouth and you're not going to try to eat me. I saw what you did to my assistant. I wasn't impressed."

To my shock, LaLee managed to look appropriately chastised. It was probably just an act. "Do they make party hats for cats?" That's what they euphemistically called muzzles in the vet's office.

Doc lifted a bushy eyebrow. "We're not going to need that, are we girl?" He gave the cat's head a little scratch and then tipped her chin up, examining her face. "Definite swelling on the left side."

LaLee wrapped her paw over the top of his arm but didn't bring out the claws.

"Let's take a look, girl." Doc's thick, practiced fingers slid LaLee's cheek high enough to expose the gum line and he gave her teeth a quick look before letting her jerk away. "Abscessed tooth. It will need to come out."

I nodded, relieved. I didn't want to admit it to myself, but I'd been afraid it was something horrible, like cancer. Ever since adopting the quirky feline, I'd been feeling like I was waiting for the other shoe to drop. "Can you do it today?"

He nodded. "I'll take her into surgery after my last appointment. One of us will call you this evening when she's ready to come home."

"Good. Thanks, Doc."

He nodded, heading to the sink to wash his hands again. "I heard about Rudolph Hortmann," he said, glancing over his shoulder. "Such a shame."

I sighed. "Sweet man."

"Murdered?" Doc turned around as he dried his hands again.

I considered side-stepping the question, but Doc's piercing gaze told me he already knew the answer to his question. Not much happened in Deer Hollow that he didn't know about.

"Strangled with his own Christmas lights," I told Doc.

His face folded in sadness. He looked down, his bushy brows lowering over brown, pebble-like eyes. "That's a darn shame." Flinging the towel into the trash, he walked over and scooped up my cat. "I didn't know the man that well. But I knew enough to know he didn't deserve to die like that."

"Any idea who might have wanted to harm him?"

Doc frowned over the question. "He kept to himself but seemed well-liked despite that. The only incident I can think about was a fuss over his truck. This was a few months ago...October maybe. A mechanic was supposed to have fixed Rudy's brakes, but they went out on him a few days after the repair. From what I heard, Rudy blamed the mechanic for the crash and subsequent damage."

"Who was the mechanic?" I asked. I couldn't help thinking that, since he ended up dead, maybe tampered brakes on Rudy's truck might have been a first shot over the bow.

"I don't know his name. All I know is that he's got a shop near Ormsville, just off Highway 46. I remember wondering why Rudy took his business all the way over there instead of just going to *The Greasy Wrench* in town."

Probably because the name sounded like something from a bad hick movie. "Did he come from that area?" I asked Doc. "Maybe he's always traded in Ormsville."

"Could be, I guess. I don't know where he lived before he moved to Deer Hollow."

Since the usually taciturn vet seemed more relaxed than normal, I decided to risk another question. "You treated Ethel Squeaks?" I asked him.

"I did. That's a nice pig."

"I'll admit it, I'm falling for her hard."

"She's with you?"

"Hal has her. We're pig-sitting until we can find her a good home. She's used to being loved and spoiled. I don't want that to change."

He nodded. "You're right about that." He lowered his brows. "Caphy meet Ethel yet?"

I winced. "No. I'm afraid Caphy might hurt her. She's never been around pigs before."

"That Pitbull doesn't have a mean bone in her body. If she didn't go after this little girl right here, she's not going to go after any animal."

I laughed. He wasn't wrong. "I need to introduce them in case Ethel ends up hanging around for a while."

"I know a couple of people who might want her. Good folks. I can give them a call?"

"Thanks, Doc."

He gave me a brusque nod. "I'll talk to you later."

"Hey, Doc," I said, stopping him before he left. "Where did Rudy get Ethel Squeaks, do you know?" I wasn't sure why I asked the question, but it suddenly seemed important.

He frowned thoughtfully. "I believe he had her when he moved here. Seems to me he got her from a friend of his." He shook his head. "I can check my notes if it's important to you. I don't think I'd have written that down but sometimes, if something strikes me as a little off, I'll add it to my record."

"Do you remember it striking you as odd?"

"I'm not sure. That would have been a few years ago now. But something about this case is nagging at me now that you've asked."

"I'd be grateful if you'd check then. If you don't mind."

"I'll do it as soon as I get five minutes."

I watched him leave, noticing a definite droop to his shoulders that usually wasn't there. He was exhausted. Hal was right, Doc needed to hire another vet. But he'd snap the head off anyone who suggested it.

That someone probably wasn't going to be me.

CHAPTER 4

*C*aphy came running when I entered the house, her pretty green eyes filled with worry. I pulled off my coat and hung it over a hook behind the door. "Hello, beautiful."

Caphy whined pitifully, jumping up to put her big paws on my arm. She sniffed me as if searching for LaLee. I carefully removed her paws before the claws snagged my sweater, kissing her on the nose. "It's okay, girl. LaLee will be home later."

Despite my words of encouragement, the house felt empty without the saucy feline and I understood why Caphy missed her. For a long time, it had just been my dog and me. But the cat had quickly insinuated herself into our hearts, and I couldn't imagine what it would be like without her.

An icy gust of wind blasted against the window in the living room that overlooked the front porch.

It was heavily marked with Caphy's nose prints, despite my having cleaned it the previous day. The pibl had probably been sitting there since I'd left, worrying about when we'd return.

I kissed the top of her head, my gaze sliding to the corner of the living room where the Christmas tree LaLee had all but demolished stood, looking a little forlorn. The tree was slightly tilted, with messy strands of lights and unevenly hung ornaments. I'd meant to fix it, so it looked pretty again, but hadn't gotten around to it with everything that had happened.

Tension tugged at me as I realized it was one more to-do item on my long list. Christmas was two days away, and I felt as if I hadn't gotten anything accomplished to prepare for it.

Well, except for baking Christmas cookies that my dog kept eating.

Sighing, I headed into the kitchen with the goal of making myself a cup of tea to warm me up. Caphy trotted along behind me. She dropped eagerly to her butt on the cold tile floor and lifted a paw, cocking her blonde head in an impossible to resist begging posture.

I opened a cookie tin and extracted one frosted sugar cookie, breaking it in half and giving her a piece. I'd have the other half with my tea while I made a list of all the stuff I needed to get done before Christmas.

A few minutes later, my notes had grown to fill half a page. Unfortunately, there was nothing on it about the tasks I needed to get done. Instead, it was filled with questions about Rudy's murder.

Number one was, *Who murdered him?* Followed by *Why was he murdered?* Did the form of murder, Christmas lights, have anything to do with the murder? Who might have had a grudge against Rudy? Who would know who might have had a grudge? Why now? Was the timing significant? Why hadn't Rudy seen his murderer? Why hadn't he fought back? Or had he?

I realized I needed to talk to Arno about the body. If Rudy had fought back when he was attacked, he might have defensive wounds that would tell a story. And if he hadn't fought hard enough to show us those wounds, did that mean he'd known his attacker?

I took my last sip of tea and sat back, frowning. Caphy's squishy head found my lap, and my fingers dug into her soft fur, scratching the preferred spot between her ears.

So many questions. So few answers.

I suddenly found it impossible to sit still. I needed to go to Hal's and check on Ethel. But it was a little early to feed her. I had time to revisit the scene of the crime. Maybe there were answers to be found there.

Or maybe the answers might find me if I only put myself in a place where I could be found.

* * *

*C*aphy romped happily in the snow, flinging icy chunks of the stuff into the air as she burrowed her nose into it, and then took off at a gallop to find the next suspicious spot needing to be uncovered.

Crunching along behind her huddled inside my coat and scarf, I briefly forgot my purpose for being at Rudy's little cabin, lost in the pure joy of watching my best friend embrace life.

The irony wasn't lost on me.

High above our heads, a squirrel chattered a strident warning, letting us know in no uncertain terms that we weren't welcome there. I squinted up at the bossy little critter, my hand shielding my eyes as a late afternoon sun turned the previously brittle day to something much easier to enjoy.

Caphy wagged her tail and barked at the squirrel, sending it chittering up the tree, no doubt thinking a few more yards of space between it and my dog were a smart move.

Knowing my dog couldn't fly, I grinned at the squirrel's precaution.

I turned back and started down the drive again. Since I'd been there the night before, multiple vehicles had beaten a two-lane path down the once impassable drive, and the sun had melted it just enough to turn it to ice.

After slipping and almost landing on my keister a few times, I decided to step into the deeper snow. It was harder to walk in but easier on my sacroiliac in the long run.

Happy snorfling brought my head up. My gaze slid toward Caphy. She was nose down, butt up, tail furiously wagging. It took me a moment to realize she was digging into the spot where Rudy had been found. I hurried over. Well, as quickly as I could given the depth of the snow. "What did you find, girl?"

She was following the trail of Rudy's death, and the thought was sobering. The sunlight had almost made the outing seem bright and carefree for a moment. The tragedy of my purpose stabbed into me with the force of a nail shot from a nail gun.

The spot was easily identified by the myriad of tracks leading to the body, circling around it, and then moving back toward the road where the ambulance had waited with a silence that spoke clearly of the finality of the return trip.

Caphy was up to her eyebrows in snow, flinging it away as her big paws shredded the hardpack, turning the place where Rudy had breathed his last breath onto its belly and giving it a sniff.

Reddish-brown soon stained the snow Caphy

was flinging and my stomach twisted with alarm. Had she uncovered blood?

But when green joined the brown, I realized it was clay that stained the snow, not old blood. Caphy had burrowed all the way through the snow and ice and had found the yard beneath it.

I stepped forward. "Leave it, girl. We don't want to dig a hole in Rudy's yard."

As I remembered it, Rudy's yard had been pristine and well-cared-for.

I'd delivered a welcome basket to him once, a few weeks after he'd moved into the area. My friend Lis had been with the Welcome Wagon then, but she'd taken a modeling job in Chicago and had asked me to fill in for her. I remembered thinking how pretty and peaceful the little cabin was, surrounded by trees with birds happily singing and the sun bathing the warm wood walls and sending the sweet scent of freshly cut lumber into the air.

I would have been more than shocked to learn what would eventually become of the home's owner. A man I remember took his welcome basket with a shy smile and a kind offer of lemonade.

Caphy barked, jumping playfully, with her muscular tail whipping from side to side. Her gaze was on something in the dirt and she hopped sideways, dropping into play posture and barking again as she batted it with a paw.

I prayed she hadn't uncovered a nest of baby

moles or something. "Caphy, leave it!" I said a bit more firmly. "What are you up to?"

At first, I saw only torn dirt and brown grass at the bottom of her excavation.

But as I crouched on the edge of the ravaged snow and peered carefully into the dirt, I saw the spec of white that was half-buried there. Using the tip of my gloved finger, I smoothed dirt away from what appeared to be a folded sheet of paper. Caphy had torn one corner of the sheet with her nails, but as I pulled it from its hidey-hole in the frozen clay, I realized it was mostly intact.

There were dark smudges on the edges. Greasy smudges. I unfolded the sheet carefully, avoiding the grease spots in case they contained useable fingerprints.

And found…

A note. Written in a large, swirly handwriting. There were five words written across the page.

I know you did it.

What did it mean, and how in the world had it ended up in the snow?

"Hello?"

My head jerked up at the questioning tone. The man stood ten yards away, a frown on his face. He looked to be in his mid-forties, probably about the same age as Rudy had been and had short-cut dark hair with gray peppering the sides. "Can I help you?"

Pushing the refolded note carefully into my

pocket, I grabbed Caphy before she could run over and say hi. Not everybody was thrilled to see a Pitbull racing toward them. Even if the only potential danger *my* pibl represented was a wet, sloppy kiss and a happy slap of a muscular tail. I clipped on her leash and straightened with a smile. "Hi. I'm working with the police. I was just taking another look around."

The man's face fell. "Rudy." He shook his head, looking sad. "I still can't believe he's gone."

I cut the distance between us, keeping my exuberant pibl on a short leash. She panted with excitement, the end of her tongue covered in dirt that had turned to mud.

"Did you know him well?"

The man shrugged, his gaze sliding to Rudy's cabin. "Well enough. Rudy kept to himself, but we'd chat over rakes and snow shovels." He smiled sadly. "He was a good neighbor."

"You live nearby?"

He nodded, pointing back the way he'd come. "Through those trees there. It's not really very far. The trees just make the homes seem isolated. We're really kind of a close-knit group."

I had trouble imagining Rudy being a social butterfly. "Can I ask your name?"

"Oh, sorry." He offered me a gloved hand and I took it. "I'm Pete Landscoff."

"Joey Fulle. Nice to meet you, Mr. Landscoff."

He pointed to the ravaged spot near the tree. "What were you digging for there?"

"Oh," I gave an embarrassed little laugh. "I'm afraid my dog was searching for something only she can identify."

"Is she a cadaver dog?"

The question gave me pause. She'd definitely found her share of bodies. But most of them had been of the fur and claw variety. Some of which she'd made into cadavers herself. "Of a sort, yes."

His lips quivered and then tightened as if he wasn't sure what the appropriate reaction would be. "Did she find anything?"

I resisted the obvious question, which was, *why do you ask*? "Just a lot of dirt and grass."

His laughter sounded strained. "Do the police think Rudy was killed?"

Knowing Deer Hollow's rumor mill like I did, I was pretty sure the man I was talking to would already have heard about the Christmas-themed murder scene, but I didn't call him on it. "The investigation is still ongoing." Which was, of course, true. But there was no question what had killed Rudy. And it seemed unlikely he'd hung *himself* with the lights. Especially since his feet had been on the ground. "Do you know of anyone who'd want to hurt Rudy?"

"Me? No, as I said, he kept to himself." He

frowned. "Come to think of it, I did hear him fighting with someone yesterday."

How convenient, I couldn't help thinking. "Do you know who it was?"

He winced. "I'm afraid so. It was the woman on the other side of those trees." He pointed to a copse of evergreens, varying sizes. I hadn't really noticed them before except in a general sense. As in, "hey, there are some trees". But I realized as I focused on them that they were planted in tidy rows, with the largest trees arrayed along what I assumed was the side boundary of Rudy's property. "A tree farm?" I asked Landscoff.

He nodded. "Rudy picked up where the previous owner left off. Those trees in the back are too big to sell, but Rudy likes...liked...the privacy they give him."

"Privacy?"

Landscoff nodded. "I take it you haven't met Lynn Dwyer?"

"No. Is she a neighbor?"

He jerked his head toward the tree farm. "She lives on the other side of those trees. I heard a chainsaw yesterday, just before the raised voices. I'm guessing Lynn cut one of Rudy's trees down again without asking. She does it every year." Landscoff shook his head. "Rudy complained to the police, but nothing ever seemed to come of it. And Lynn does no wrong, ever. As far as she's concerned, Rudy owed her those trees. Though nobody's quite sure why that would be and Lynn's characteristically vague about it." Landscoff's gaze slid toward the structure I could just barely see through the trees. "If I was looking for somebody with a grudge against Rudy, she'd be the first person I'd question."

* * *

A moment later, I said goodbye to Rudy's neighbor, but not before asking him if he'd be around in case I thought of any more questions. He seemed perfectly willing to make himself available, but there was something in his gaze, a shrewd calculation when it sifted over the cabin and the property that made me uncomfortable.

I made a mental note to try to find out more about Mr. Landscoff, and Caphy and I started across the snow, into the tree farm. The sharp aroma of crushed pine needles permeated the space and the evergreens cut the occasional brisk breeze to nothing. It was pleasant inside the trees, sheltered and sunny so that it felt at least ten degrees warmer.

We hadn't gone far before my nose picked up the scent of sawdust. I found the slender stump a few rows inside the boundary of the farm, at the center of a pretty row of long-needled pines. I ran my fingers over the rough cut of the stump, noting the spike spearing upward from one edge as if the tree had been cut to a point and then just shoved over to break it free.

Like the person cutting it down had been in a hurry.

Had Lynn gotten caught in the act of stealing the tree?

Caphy had lost interest in the stump and was sniffing the snow heading out of the farm. I followed her, watching as she jammed her smooshy snout into the frozen white stuff and came out sneezing. She reared back and barked at the hole she'd made and I tensed. "If you're trying to roust a mouse or something, I pass, pretty girl. Not interested."

I didn't mind outdoor critters of any kind. Mostly. But I was less than fond of having them jump out at me and scurry over my feet.

Nothing came out of the hole. When Caphy dove at it again, her claws ripped the snow cover off and I saw what must have made her sneeze.

Pine needles. Lots of them. I crouched down and used my gloved hands to pull the top layer of snow off, finding more needles as I moved forward and repeated the motion. After a minute, I realized I was following a trail of the things.

Like somebody had dragged a freshly cut tree along the snow.

I straightened as we passed the last row of trees and my gaze found an ugly brown house hunkered down amid the pristine white snow. That was where the snow-covered path was leading us.

And the woman standing on the porch wearing a hostile glare and holding a shotgun in her badly chapped hands was no doubt the infamous Lynn.

CHAPTER 5

I tugged Caphy close, trying to pull her behind me as the woman lifted the shotgun, the scowl on her fleshy face deepening. "What are you doin' on my property?"

Funny how the woman suddenly seemed concerned about property rights when someone stepped onto *her* land. She hadn't seemed to care when she apparently went over to Rudy's and took one of his trees. I bit my tongue against the desire to tell her just that. I was pretty sure if I did, Hal and Arno would be searching for my body until the snow melted in the spring. "I'm Joey Fulle. I'm working with the police." I left it there, hoping she'd think twice about murdering my dog and me if she believed the police knew I was there. "Deputy Willager asked me to talk to Rudy Hortmann's neighbors."

"About what?" She didn't lower the shotgun, but I saw the first crack in her glower as curiosity replaced some of the hostility.

"Did you see or hear anything last night?"

"A lot of wind and snow. What else would I hear and see?" Her voice was hostile, but she lowered the shotgun and cocked a hip. An icy wind scoured the ground, sending snow spiraling up and sweeping the gray-brown strands of her frizzy hair aloft. She didn't look cold. Though she certainly wasn't dressed for the weather. I eyed the loose flannel pants and light sweater she wore, her feet covered in slippers with fleece around the tops. A delicate chain supporting a silver cross between her large breasts was the only jewelry she wore.

Her words sank in and I wondered, was it possible she didn't know about Rudy? "Your neighbor, Rudy Hortmann was murdered last night. We believe the person who killed him left his car on the road in front of your place." That was pure speculation on my part since all the driveways were covered over with snow, but I was pretty sure, judging by the distance past Rudy's drive where we'd seen evidence of another vehicle, that it was close to Lynn's driveway. "Did you see any headlights you couldn't explain? See anybody walking across your property?"

"You think I hang out by the windows all night? I got better things to do."

I glanced around the tumbledown property, noting the snow-covered mounds of stuff all around the yard and the carport doing a poor job of keeping the snow from blanketing a rusted powder blue and white truck. Judging by the ten inches of snow on the car's roof and hood, Lynn hadn't taken it out since the storm started.

Though she wouldn't need to drive over to Rudy's to kill him.

"I noticed a tree had been cut down over there," I told her, keeping my expression as neutral as I could. "There are drag marks leading to your property. Did you cut down one of Rudy's trees?"

Her gaze slid briefly to the sparkling multi-colored lights I could see through one of the windows in the careworn home and then quickly away, turning speculative. "What of it?"

I shrugged, surprised. I'd expected her to deny it. "Did you and Rudy fight about that tree?"

"Rudy don't get ta have an opinion about my takin' a tree or two from there. They planted that farm five feet over my property line. I have a right ta take any trees I want from there."

She seemed pretty sure about that. Enough to inspire me to look into her claim. "One of your neighbors told me you and Rudy had an argument yesterday. Is that true?"

Her scowl deepened, turning her fleshy face pugnacious. "You talkin' about Landscoff?" She blew a raspberry. "He's one ta talk. Him and Rudy barely talked to each other."

"Why's that?"

"Everybody knows he wanted that property for himself. He's tried ta buy it out from under Rudy a dozen times. But that guy wasn't givin' an inch."

"Rudy refused to sell it to him?" That seemed obvious, but I wanted to keep the woman talking.

"Yep. He was dug into that place like the roots that little pig of his favored. He wasn't sellin' ta nobody." She shrugged. "I didn't mind him so much. I liked the pig. But he should'a given me a cut of his tree farm since they'd planted some of it on my land."

"Do you have a survey that proves the farm had leeched over the boundary?" I asked.

"Yeah. I do. I showed it to him too. He said it didn't matter because the survey he got done when he bought the place included the tree line." She shook her head. "I couldn't afford ta take him to court over it."

I nodded. "Maybe now that he's gone, you can get your land back." I watched her carefully, gauging her reaction. She didn't disappoint.

A shrewd look turned her pale gaze hard, brittle like the air around us. "Yeah. Don't think I haven't considered that."

* * *

*D*eer Hollow Realtors was located in an old brick building whose front was stained black with age and soot. Long, meandering cracks severed the mortar between the bricks in several spots, and were unattractively filled with what looked like instant concrete. The porch was still warped with age as it had been the last time I was there, and the supports beneath it still looked bent and rickety.

The woman who looked up from her computer when I entered was in her forties, plump and pretty in a careless way. I gave her a quick smile. "Hi, Madge."

The realtor stood and offered me her hand, "Hey, Joey. It's nice to see you again." Her eyes took on a speculative light. "Please tell me you're here to list your beautiful house."

Madge Watson and her now-deceased partner, Penney Sellers...long story...had been lusting after my home since the pair moved into Deer Hollow from Indianapolis. Madge and I were at loggerheads over the issue. She was as determined to sell it out from under me as I was to hold onto it. But it was a friendly loggerheads. If there was such a thing.

Her smile was warm and resigned when I told her I wasn't there to list. "What can I help you with?"

"I'm here about Rudolph Robert Hortmann's property out on Goose Down Road."

Her pale blue gaze widened. "I heard he was murdered."

There was no point denying the murder. The rumor mill in Deer Hollow not only functioned at lightning speed, it was also pretty accurate, and we all knew it. "Unfortunately, yes. Hal and I are helping Arno with some of the legwork."

The woman's blue gaze sparked with interest at mention of Hal. "How is your extremely handsome boyfriend, hon? Is he enjoying his new home?"

"He loves it. I'm happy to report that he's spending a lot of time in it." I grinned. Madge's partner Penney had been Hal's realtor when he'd bought the battered-down old cabin on the property adjoining mine. The place had once belonged to my uncle through friendship rather than birth, and it had been a mess when he'd bought it. Hal had since turned it into a snugly pleasant home that he lived in whenever he wasn't in Indianapolis, helping his brother Cal Amity with their Private Investigation business there.

"That's good. I'm glad."

I nodded. "I'm here because I interviewed a couple of Rudy's neighbors today and they both seemed very interested in his property."

She nodded. "Yes. Pete Landscoff has made several offers, but Mr. Hortmann wasn't interested in selling."

"Did you work with Pete on those offers?"

Deer Hollow Realtors was the only realtor in Deer Hollow itself. But there were other offices in the surrounding areas that could have taken on Landscoff's business.

"I did. All five times. Unfortunately, I wasn't here yet when he offered on the property before Mr. Hortmann bought it, so I can't tell you about that offer."

"How badly did Mr. Landscoff want that property?" I asked.

Her expression turned shrewd. I realized that my speculations about Rudy's neighbor would be a key topic in the rumor mill before the sun set on Deer Hollow. "You're asking me if he would have killed for it?"

I nodded.

"That's a tough question. Judging by the offers Landscoff made for the property, he wanted it badly."

"They were generous?"

She nodded. "More than it was worth and then some. But Mr. Hortmann wasn't interested in selling. He finally threatened me that he was going to get a restraining order for this office if we presented him with another offer."

"Could he have done that?"

"I doubt it. Unless he could prove that my emails were harassing, and I assure you they weren't. But I told Mr. Landscoff I wouldn't present any more offers anyway. I don't need that kind of bad feeling. It's hard enough to run this office by myself as it is."

A weary look passed through her expression and I felt bad for her. "Have you looked into replacing Penney?"

She nodded. "So far, I haven't found anybody who wants to move out to bumpkinville." She paled as soon as she said the word. "I'm sorry. I hope that doesn't offend you, Joey. It wasn't meant to."

"Not at all. I'm happy to be a country bumpkin." I gave her a sincere smile. "But I can certainly understand that this lifestyle isn't for everybody."

She nodded again. "I'm looking into luring someone from the local realtors, but very few of them have the skills I'm looking for. I'd even be willing to train someone, but most of them seem resistant to being retrained."

I could understand that too. Knowing how country folks thought, they'd probably resent the "big city" realtor coming in and telling them how to sell houses. "I'll keep my eyes and ears open," I told her. "If I hear of anybody who might be interested, I'll send them your way."

She reached out and patted my hand. "Thanks, hon. You're too good to me."

"I'm happy to help."

Madge frowned thoughtfully. "I did get a strange call on the Hortmann property yesterday. I'd forgotten about it until you mentioned Landscoff."

"Pete Landscoff called about buying the property yesterday?"

"No." She shook her head. "It was a woman. She wanted to know the value of the property. I told her I couldn't give that information out unless it was my listing. Even then, I wouldn't have. I didn't tell her that. But I did tell her the information was searchable online."

"Did she give you her name?"

"No. I tried to get it, I assure you." She laughed. "All I can tell you is she was rude and demanding. As desperate as I am, I wouldn't have taken her on as a client even if she'd asked me to. I don't need those kinds of headaches right now."

Her story reminded me of Lynn Dwyer's claims. "I spoke to the neighbor on the other side of Rudy and she claims his tree farm is encroaching on her property line. Have you heard anything about that?"

Madge shook her head. "No. But, like I said, I wasn't here when that property was sold to Mr. Hortmann."

"Do you think the sale went through this office?"

Realization filled her expression. "Yes. I'll bet it did. I can check the older records. I bought the whole business from the previous realtor, and all of her records should still be here. They're in a file cabinet in the back." She grimaced. "It's quite a mess. I understood after seeing them why the woman lost control of her business." She shook her head.

"Would you mind looking through them for me?" I asked. "I know it's asking a lot."

She shook her head and I thought she was saying no. But then she smiled. "I've been meaning to sort through those files anyway. I'll let you know if I find anything. It could take a couple of days, though."

I gave her an impulsive hug. "Thanks so much, Madge." Her cheeks pinkened with embarrassment. "It's nothing at all. I owe you my life. It's the least I can do."

"You don't owe me your life."

"Yes. I do. This small favor won't come near to paying you back, Joey. But it's a start."

I wanted to deny her claim, but I knew it wouldn't do any good. She wanted to believe we'd saved her and that was what she'd believe. Madge had gotten herself in the middle of a murder investigation Hal and I were pursuing and had nearly died. Hal and I were only remotely involved in her being found before the poison she'd been dosed with killed her.

"We're just really glad you're okay."

She nodded. "I'll get back to you with what I learn, hon. And let me know if you find someone to join this office. I'd trust anybody you sent my way to be good people."

CHAPTER 6

I checked the steaks and poked the potatoes I had baking on skewers on the grill, my breath making soft plumes against the chilly night air.

Stomping my feet against the stones of the patio, I headed back inside. I closed the door and brushed my half-frozen hands together, warming them. LaLee rubbed against my calves, happy to be home despite the fact that I'd taken her to the vet in the first place. Figuring that once she got over being glad, she'd go back to mad again, I decided to enjoy the temporary truce while it lasted. I bent down to scratch between the perky, dark brown ears. "Hey, pretty girl. How's your mouth feeling?"

She hissed, rearing back and swatting my hand with unleashed claws.

And there it went.

Snatching my hand away, I watched her lope from the room, tail high and twitching.

It had all been a trap. And I'd fallen for it.

Stupid, Joey. Stupid, stupid Joey.

The front door opened and closed, and Hal called out. I tugged off my coat and hung it over the back of one of the chairs at the table near the patio door. "I'm in the kitchen!"

He carried the icy scent of the outdoors in with him, stopping to place a soft kiss on my lips. "It smells delicious in here. What are you cooking?"

"The cooking is all outside, I'm afraid. And now that you're here..." I waggled my brows.

"You're grilling? It's twenty-five degrees out there."

"I was in the mood for steak and potatoes." I tugged on the neckline of his crisp, blue button-down shirt. "You don't mind, do you?"

He kissed me again. "Happens I was craving steak myself." His nostrils flared. "But something definitely smells good in here."

I sighed. "I'm baking more Christmas cookies. Caphy got into another box today while I was gone. I put the rest in the freezer so she can't get to them."

He nodded, heading to the fridge. "Beer or wine?"

"Wine, please."

He got himself a bottle of beer and grabbed a

wine glass from a glass-fronted cabinet near the sink. "How'd the girl's vet appointment go? Did she lose a tooth?"

"She did. It was abscessed."

"She mad at you?"

I held my hand up and showed him the scratches. "She was acting friendly, so I let my guard down."

Hal made a sad face and grabbed my hand, kissing the scratches. "She's something else."

My timer went off, and I hurried over to check the sugar cookies. The edges were perfectly browned, so I pulled them from the oven and slid the next batch inside, resetting the timer.

"Speaking of something else, did you check on Ethel?"

His expression tightened.

I misread his reaction, alarm making me ask, "Is she okay?"

"She's fine. But she's very — needy is the right word, I guess. I felt bad leaving her again."

I took the wine he handed me. "Thanks. I stopped over there earlier and spent some time with her."

He nodded. "I'm thinking she's used to having an almost constant companion. I don't think Rudy left his house much."

I frowned. "What did he do for a living?" I asked.

Hal shook his head. "No idea. Something with

computers, I think. Whatever it was, he worked from home."

I thought about the Ethel problem. "I guess we could spend more time at your place until we find her a home."

He sat down and sipped his beer as Caphy jogged into the kitchen to greet him. He reached to pet her, and she hit the ground, going belly up so he could scratch her cookie-filled belly. "If we do that, Caphy will be lonely."

I noticed he didn't suggest LaLee might be lonely. I was thinking the cat was happiest when she was alone. Still, she did always seem to gravitate to whatever room we were in, so it could all be an act.

I sighed. "We probably need to bite the bullet and introduce Ethel to Caphy."

Hal's face split in a wide grin. "If you insist." He was out of his chair and hurrying toward the front of the house before I even registered that he'd moved.

I blinked in surprise. "Hal?"

"Be right back!" he called out.

Realization hit me when I heard the front door close. I started toward the front of the house, Caphy trotting at my heels. A plaintive yowl met me at the bottom of the stairs and I glanced up the stairwell to the spot where LaLee lay, her tail angrily snapping. "I said I was sorry," I told her for the tenth time. She jerked to her feet and stalked up the stairs, disappearing through my bedroom door. "Judgmental darn cat," I murmured.

The front door opened and Ethel shot through, all but dragging Hal behind her on the end of the leash.

Caphy yelped, went straight up in the air, and shot up the stairs as the pig skidded happily to a stop.

I gave Hal a look.

He did have the good sense to flinch. "I just couldn't leave her there alone again."

My heart melted a little bit. "You left her in the car? It's way too cold."

He shook his head, pointing to the hot pink and black striped sweater Ethel was wearing. "She had her sweater on, and I made her a nest of blankets. Plus, I left the car running and the heater on."

I almost laughed. The pig had probably been warmer than me. "Okay," I finally said. "A little warning would have been nice. Caphy may never come down again."

Hal nodded toward the landing above. "I wouldn't worry about that. She's too curious not to want to check out the pig."

Ethel snorfled my shins and pressed her solid body into my legs, her tail a happy whirligig beneath her sweater. I couldn't resist giving her a scratch. "Hi, pretty girl. Were you lonesome?"

She did a funny little dance and pressed into me again.

"Joey," Hal murmured softly. He nodded past my shoulder.

I turned to find Caphy sitting on the bottom step, her pretty green gaze locked warily on the pig. "Hey, Caphy, girl. This is Ethel." I reached out and touched Caphy's squishy face. She ran her wide tongue over my fingers but didn't take her eyes from the pig. "She's our friend."

Caphy definitely didn't look like she believed me.

I hooked my fingers around her collar and gave it a gentle tug. "Come here, pretty girl."

She let me tug her closer, hunching against me as I crouched to enfold her in one arm. Ethel's snout quivered as she scented my pibl. She moved slowly, carefully, as if she understood my dog's reluctance.

Caphy's tail gave a quick, uncertain wag as Ethel's snout came close. When the pig didn't attack, her tail swept the floor a bit more enthusiastically. She leaned close to sniff Ethel in return.

A minute later, the two were circling each other, getting the lay of the land in a much calmer fashion.

The timer for my cookies brought me out of my crouch. I headed into the kitchen and Caphy came with me, tail happily wagging. Hal kept Ethel on the leash as they followed.

"Well, that went about as well as can be expected," I told him as I pulled cookies from the oven.

"Yeah," He said, retrieving his beer. "But we haven't introduced her to LaLee yet."

I sighed. "Spoilsport. How'd your outing with Arno go?"

"Not good. The homeless guy was cleared by the local cops because he'd been locked in a homeless shelter at the time the girl was killed. There were a dozen witnesses who verified his alibi, one of which was the priest from the Catholic church that sponsors the home. In addition, the man has no history of owning a gun. Nobody's ever seen him holding one. And there were zero points of intersection between him and the victim."

"Then why was he a suspect in the first place?"

"Apparently he was seen with a young co-ed who resembled the victim earlier that night. She gave him twenty dollars and told him to get a meal with it. Fortunately for that coed, she wasn't the girl who was killed."

"A complete dead end," I said.

"Yes, and no. Part of investigating a murder is eliminating suspects. We can now safely eliminate that one."

"Well, I talked to the neighbors on either side of Rudy today, as well as Madge at Deer Hollow Realtors."

He cocked a brow. "You were busy."

I filled him in on what I'd learned from the two neighbors.

"There's definitely motive there. Especially for Lynn."

"I agree." I suddenly remembered the note Caphy had found. "I almost forgot!" I reached into my jeans pocket. "Caphy dug this up in the spot where Rudy died. I'm thinking it might be from the killer."

Hal's eyes went wide. "It absolutely could be. I'll give it to Arno and he can have someone compare the handwriting to that of all our suspects." He frowned. "I'm surprised his people didn't find it when they moved the body."

"I actually have a theory on that. The note was buried under a thin layer of ice. Since it was white, I don't think anyone would have noticed it. Caphy smelled it under there and dug through the ice."

"Okay, but how'd it get under Rudy? If he'd been holding it, why was there a layer of ice between him and the note?"

I shrugged. "Maybe he dropped it in the struggle. When he fell on the snow, it melted from his body heat and then refroze?"

"That's as good a theory as any," Hal agreed. He gave me a proud smile. "That's some good investigating, PI Joey."

I couldn't help grinning. "Did you and Arno talk to the mechanic in Ormsville?"

"The shop was closed by the time Arno and I got there. Arno has to be in court tomorrow. Would you like to take a ride over there with me?"

I would, actually. I'd like that a lot. And I would have told him so, but Caphy and Ethel decided to take off running through the house in that moment. And Hal and I spent the next several minutes trying to catch them before they totally trashed my house.

ike's Mechanics didn't look like much from the outside. A young girl sat on a weather-worn bench outside, sipping a bottle of diet soda and crunching chips. She looked to be in her early twenties and her pale, thin face was streaked with grease. She tugged on a heavy chain with a gothic style cross on it and watched us as we moved past, her gaze only skimming away when I returned her perusal.

As we stepped into the small garage, my impressions didn't improve much. The place had no office area. It was located in an old clapboard building whose exterior had once been white but was badly in need of a paint job. The interior was about the size of a 3-car garage, but half again as deep.

It smelled like stale oil and gasoline. Nearly every surface was covered by small engines and parts.

The man standing at a plywood worktable in the back glanced our way as we came inside. He was average height, lean beneath the dirty coveralls he wore, and had a mop of greasy hair that looked black but might have been a lighter color if it was clean. "I'll be with you in a minute," he said in a voice made raspy by too many cigarettes.

I skimmed my gaze over the contents of the place, arching a brow at Hal. Mike's didn't appear to be a car repair shop at all. It looked like a small engine repair shop. Which made me wonder why Rudy had brought his truck there for brakes.

The man dropped a greasy wrench to the tabletop and turned, rubbing his hands on a rag that was liberally splotched with oily black stains.

When he smiled, he showcased a mouth full of yellowed and crooked teeth. He smelled like an unpleasant mix of gasoline and stale tobacco. "How can I help you, folks?"

"Are you Mike?" Hal asked.

The mechanic nodded. "That's me."

Hal offered him a quick glance of his PI's license. "I'm Hal Amity, Amity Private Investigations. This is my partner, Joey."

Mike offered me his hand. I grimaced before I could stop myself.

He gave the greasy thing a perplexed look before it seemed to occur to him it wasn't fit for pleasantries. "Sorry. It's been a busy morning."

Hal nodded. "Business is good?"

"It is. Better than I deserve." He gave an odd laugh and shook his head, clearly not comfortable dealing with people. Without asking if we'd mind, he pulled a pack of cigarettes out of the pocket of his coveralls and lit it, drawing deeply and blowing the smoke from the side of his mouth so it wouldn't smack us in the face. "Do you need an engine repaired?"

"We're following up on a suspicious death in Deer Hollow. Maybe you heard about it? The victim's name was Rudy-Bob Hortmann."

The man's gaze slid assessingly to me and then back to Hal. He coughed wetly. "Yeah, I heard about it."

"We understand Rudy was a customer of yours."

Mike shrugged, inhaling and blowing smoke out in a slow swirl before answering. "He occasionally brought stuff here." He narrowed his gaze. "Is this about the brakes? 'Cause my insurance covered the damage. I thought we put that behind us."

Hal nodded. "We're just looking at all possible avenues." He looked around. "I don't see any other vehicles here."

The man took Hal's inference and bristled. "I got lots of experience with engines of all kinds. I worked in a brake shop in Indy for years."

"Still, it seems a strange place for Rudy Hortmann to bring a truck for brakes. Can you tell me why he chose you over a mechanic who did that kind of thing on a regular basis?"

I watched Mike carefully, noting the way his gaze skimmed to the left before he responded. He held his cigarette up in front of his face as if hiding behind it.

"I gave him a good deal."

"You knew each other?"

After a slight hesitation, Mike nodded. "Me and Rudy go way back. We grew up in Ormsville and went to school together until college."

"You went to a different school?" I asked, smiling to soften the invasive question.

Something like anger skimmed through his pale brown gaze. "I didn't go to college. I'm not that fancy, I guess." His laugh was probably meant to be self-deprecating, but it just came off as bitter.

"Rudy brought you work over the years?" Hal asked. I could tell he thought something didn't smell right, but I had no idea what he was digging for.

Mike dropped the cigarette and ground it into the oil-covered concrete with his boot. "If you're implying he felt sorry for me, don't. Me and Rudy was friends. We helped each other out."

"What happened with the brakes," Hal asked.

Mike's face tightened. "Them brakes was fine when he left here. If Rudy's been murdered, maybe he pissed somebody off. It wouldn't be the first time murder's happened around here."

A strange thing for him to say. But I chalked it up to his basic social awkwardness.

"No, it wouldn't." Hal nodded. "Did you ever meet a girl named Tannie Bishopson?"

The man frowned, his cheek twitching slightly. "No, who's she?"

"Student at IU. She was shot a few years back. Rudy had the weapon that killed her in his home."

Mike's eyes went wide. His mouth fell open before he caught himself, scrubbing a hand through his shaggy hair. "That's not possible." He looked up at Hal. "You think Rudy killed that girl?"

"I was wondering what *you* thought," Hal responded. "Was Rudy capable of that kind of thing? Had there been any...incidents...with women growing up?"

Mike started to shake his head but stopped. "There was this one girl. I can't remember her name. She was a cheerleader, really popular." He reached for the pack of cigarettes, lighting another one before continuing his thought. "She claimed he tussled with her under the bleachers once, tried to cop a feel, you know." Mike shrugged. "We didn't think nothing of it. We were walkin' hormones in those days." He laughed sourly. "I never thought Rudy..." He shook his head, dragging deeply on his cigarette.

"Is there anybody else who could have hurt that girl? Did Rudy ever talk about her to you?"

"Like I said, I didn't go to school. Rudy wouldn't have talked to me about anything having to do with college. It was kind of a sore point with me."

Hal gave him a business card. "If you think of anything else, will you call?"

"Sure. But I won't. I don't know nothin' about no girl gettin' killed."

Me thinks he dost protest too much, I couldn't help thinking.

We started out of the shop. Mike hailed us as Hal reached for the doorknob. "Hey, if you see the girl out there, shoo her on inside, will ya?"

Hal lifted a hand as I scooted through in front of him.

The girl wasn't sitting on the bench when we came outside. But as we headed toward where we'd parked Hal's SUV, a slight figure pushed off from a rusty sedan with an oil leak. She was petite, with well-formed arms highlighted by a snug turtleneck in a pale pink color. The coverall sleeves were rolled to her elbows and the hems were rolled to the tops of her small sneakers. She wore a ratty red stocking cap over her shoulder-length dark brown hair, a greasy IU emblem adorning the center.

She looked to be about twenty-one years old. The pleasant scent of cinnamon came with her as she moved near. Probably from the gloss on her full lips.

I stopped, reaching for Hal's arm to halt him.

"Hey," I said, giving the girl a smile. "I think Mike's looking for you."

She slid a quick look toward the smeared glass of the front window, her expression filled with disgust. When she refocused on me, the expression turned vulnerable, making her look ten years younger. "You were askin' about Tannie Bishopson?"

"We were," Hal responded, turning to face the girl. "Did you know her?"

She shrugged. "Not personally. She was a junior. I was just a freshman."

"But you know what happened to her?"

"She was killed. Everybody knows that. Right before Christmas." The way she said that last made me wonder if the time of year made it somehow worse in her mind.

I realized the young woman was going to make us extract the information she so clearly wanted to impart one piece of a time. She was reticent, I guessed. But something inside her wouldn't let her just walk away. "But you know something beyond what everybody knows, don't you?" I asked.

Only the briefest hesitation preceded her nod. "The school covered up what really happened. They didn't want the police to know the truth."

"Why not?" Hal asked, but I suspected he knew why not. I was pretty sure I did too. "They're protecting somebody," I offered gently.

She glanced toward the window again, her expression thoughtful. She still clearly struggled with what she knew.

I misread her glance. "Was Mike involved?"

She blinked in surprise. "Mike?" She snorted out a laugh. "I doubt it. He's not smart enough to get away with it."

I winced at her brutality. She clearly didn't respect her boss. Or even like him, judging by the twist of her lips as she glanced his way. "Then, who?"

"There was this professor..."

I almost sighed. Wasn't there always? It was such a cliché, but it was a cliché that played itself out over and over again at campuses across the country.

"You think one of the staff at IU killed Tannie Bishopson?" Hal asked.

Chewing her lip, she said, "It wasn't like you're thinking. It wasn't a sexual thing. They were friends. But Professor Freir's wife didn't like Tannie. I guess she didn't trust her husband."

Hal nodded. I could see by the expression on his face that he didn't believe in the friendship angle. But the jealous wife, aspect to the girl's story definitely had promise. "His name was Freir?"

"Yes. But you can't talk to him."

"Why not?" I asked. If the school tried to stop us. we'd just find a way around them.

"Because he's dead. He died not too long after Tannie did."

* * *

"*B*randon Freir was killed in a parachuting accident," Hal told me.

Nibbling on a raw carrot, I leaned over his shoulder to read the article. "Hmm, I guess that could be murder."

"Only if the wife knew how to make a parachute malfunction," Hal said. He frowned. "And, since she's now suing the instructor at the jumping school, that seems cold-blooded at best and unlikely at worst."

"Why? I asked, throwing Caphy and Ethel a carrot. The pibl caught hers midair and then turned to try to grab Ethel's. But the pig swung her butt around to block Caphy as she happily chewed hers.

Perched on the back of the couch where Hal was working, LaLee looked down her nose at the other two animals, clearly believing that raw vegetables were too pedestrian for her elegant palate.

"If she killed the husband herself, it would be foolhardy for her to push herself into the investigation. It would be the smarter play to keep a low profile. Play the grieving wife."

I dropped onto the couch next to him. "So his death probably isn't tied to Tannie's."

"Not unless there's another angle we're missing," Hal agreed. "The police signed off on accidental death for Freir and never even questioned the wife, despite the girl's murder, which tells me it was a pretty clear-cut case of accidental. Apparently, Mrs. Freir was in Indianapolis visiting family when Tannie was killed. She had several witnesses to back up her alibi. But, I'll have Arno check into connections between Rudy and Mrs. Freir, just in case."

Placing his laptop onto the coffee table, he pulled me across his lap, wrapping his arms around my waist. "You smell sugary."

I grinned. "I've been frosting cookies."

"Mmm," he said, touching his lips to mine. "Any broken ones?"

"No." I kissed him on the tip of his long, Greek nose. "And don't try that trick of breaking one so you have to eat it. I'm on to your ruses. You're as bad as Caphy."

He gave me a mock look of horror, one hand flat against his chest as if I'd mortally wounded him. "I can't believe you just said that. Nobody...certainly not a humble gastronomist like me...could deign to ever reach the same level of begging dexterity as the pibl. Nobody."

I twisted my lips to hold back a smile. "You're not wrong." I kissed his lips, lingering long enough to let him know I was glad he was mine. And when I broke it, I offered him something almost as sweet. "Okay, you earned one cookie for the five-dollar word. But only one."

I headed into the kitchen, Hal right on my heels and a hopeful pibl bringing up the rear.

"If I'd known it would be that easy," Hal said, "I'd have broken out the five-dollar words days ago. Maybe even a ten-dollar word or two."

I let my giggle escape. "Nice try. I'm no longer in the market for big words."

My cell rang as I indicated the lines of frosted cookies on the counter. Seeing it was my friend, Lis, I answered. "Hey, girlfriend! Are you home for Christmas?" I held one finger up to Hal and he gave me an angelic smile which made my brows arch.

He was totally going to steal more than one cookie. And since I couldn't see his legs from the knees down because of all the critters smashed around them, it was a pretty good bet I'd be baking more cookies later.

Sigh…

"I am. I'm at Sonny's. I wondered if you guys wanted to meet me for an early dinner. Arno said he might stop by."

I glanced at my boyfriend, whose lips were covered in cookie crumbs, and my pibl, whose mouth was covered in frosting, to the pig, who apparently really got into her food because she had a smear of blue frosting across one ear, and said. "We'd love to. I'm the only one who'll probably be hungry though, if the sad state of the latest batch of Christmas cookies is any indication."

"Oh! Bring me one. Just *one*, Joey. You know I'll eat them all if you bring more."

I smiled. "Just one. I promise. We'll see you in a bit."

CHAPTER 8

"*Y*ou *said* only one," I told my best friend, laughing.

Lis shoved her hands through her short, choppy auburn hair and groaned in despair. But she wasted no time reaching inside the cardboard holiday box to break off a chunk of the dinner-plate-sized cookie I'd baked that morning in anticipation of her "one cookie" rule.

She closed her eyes in sheer pleasure as she popped the bite between her lips. "Thank you for ignoring the 'one cookie' rule," she moaned.

"That's what friends are for," I responded, grinning. My friend, the supermodel was tall and almost too skinny, with a rigid eating regimen she seldom broke. I was happy to see her bend the rules and treat herself for once. "Besides, you have no idea how hard it was to keep that cookie away from all my chow hounds today."

Lis arched a perfect brow. "LaLee likes cookies too?"

"Not a chance. I suppose if I made her a fish-flavored cookie…" I grimaced. "But Caphy's already gone through a couple dozen of the ones I baked for gifts. And her sidekick…" I slid Hal a look.

Lis looked shocked. "Hal? Your temple!"

My boyfriend liked to tell us he considered his body a temple, and he honored it by feeding it healthy food. He mostly did just that. But I was starting to realize being around the ultimate country bumpkin and her comfort-food ways was wearing him down.

Hal patted his flat belly. "I might have overindulged just a titch."

I snorted.

The door to the diner opened, and the bell jangled cheerfully, the red-velvet bow someone had tied there a happy spot of color above the door.

I rubbed my sweater-covered arms as an icy draft flew across the small diner and looked up as Deputy Arno Willager, Lis's favorite villager, entered on the front end of another draft as if he'd been blown inside.

He looked around and spotted us, stomping snow off his boots before heading our way.

Hal stood up and shook his hand. "Deputy, did you get that information on Mrs. Freir?"

Arno nodded. "There was no connection between her and Rudy that we could find." He hung his coat on the hook embedded at the end of the booth, eyeing the bench beside Lis. She gave him a smile, scooting over and patting the torn and taped red vinyl. "Have a seat." She looked at Hal. "Let the man get settled before jumpin' on him about business, Hal."

My PI shook his head and sat, draping an arm around my shoulders. "Sorry. I'm a horrible person."

Lis winked at Hal. He smiled.

Arno sat down, his gaze finding the giant cookie. He looked at me. "You baked this?"

"How could you tell?" I asked with a grin.

"Maybe because there's a big pawprint on the icing."

I held up my hands. "It's not real. I swear."

"You mean you didn't set it down on the floor and have her stand on it?" Arno asked, reaching for the broken corner and getting his hand slapped for his trouble.

"No, but that's an excellent idea for next year."

"Don't worry," Hal said, signaling the waitress. "Caphy definitely got involved in the baking."

"Mostly she just got involved in the eating," I said, wincing.

"Well, let me go on record as not wanting any

paw impressions in my cookies this year." Arno declared.

"Who says you're gonna get cookies this year, Scrooge?" I asked.

He chuckled. "Thank goodness you're much too kind-hearted to exclude me just because I'm cranky."

"It's true," I agreed easily. "You're darn lucky."

Nodding agreement, Arno looked up and smiled as Max, the owner of Sonny's Diner, came over with an order pad. "I'd like coffee, Max."

She nodded. "Y'all ready to order?"

"I think we're going to need a few minutes," Lis said.

"You got it. I'll be right back with that coffee." Max jammed her pencil back into the ratty tangle of yellow-white hair piled on top of her head and shuffled toward the coffee maker.

Quick as a wink, Arno reached over and broke a chunk of cookie off before Lis could stop him.

"Hey!"

"So sorry, my hand slipped."

Lis covered the box and pushed it away from Arno. Sipping from her cup of tea, she grew serious. "I can't believe Rudy's dead."

It was her way of letting us know it was okay to talk about it. She'd only been half teasing when she shut Hal down about the investigation. I knew she hated dwelling on such sad news at Christmas time.

Lis was a total sap about the holidays. It was her favorite time of year.

But real life happened.

"He was a really nice man," I said. Though the more we dug into his life, the more I wondered if that was true.

"Do you have any idea who might have done this to him?" she asked Arno.

"A couple. So far, nothing's panning out."

"What do you know about the neighbors on either side of him," I asked Arno. "I spoke to them yesterday. They both had designs on his property."

He nodded. "Hal dropped by the station this morning with the letter you found and filled me in. Lynn Dwyer fights with everybody in town. If you think I'm crabby, she's ten times worse. She's only lived here about two and a half years, but she's managed to annoy almost everyone since. I wouldn't be surprised to hear she and Rudy didn't get along. But I don't have anything at all that says she's violent. No record of anything. Not even a parking ticket."

"How about Pete Landscoff?" I asked him.

"Mr. Landscoff is a nice guy," Arno said, as if that was what I'd been asking. "He's well-liked, follows the rules, both legal and social, and seems to have been a pretty good neighbor too."

"Except for continually trying to buy the property out from under Rudy. Madge over at Deer

Hollow Realtors said he insisted on offering for the house anonymously several times just in case Rudy might change his mind."

"That's definitely strange behavior," Hal agreed. "But it's a long way from there to murder."

Arno shook his head. "I just don't see it."

"What does he do?" Hal asked.

"Do? You mean professionally? I think he writes for some of the bigger newspapers around the country. He might have a book out too." He shrugged. "I think it might be a political thriller."

Lis tugged the cover off her cookie box and broke off another chunk, offering it to Arno. "I didn't know Rudy well. I've only met him a couple of times. But we spoke a few months ago. I was picking mom up from the hospital," she glanced at me. "When she did that stint as a volunteer?"

"Reading to the kids in the cancer ward," I nodded, a wave of sadness sliding through me as I remembered the pictures she'd taken of the kids in the ward. I couldn't help comparing those faces to the bright smiles of the kids sitting on Rudy's red-velvet-clad lap the other night. The two images didn't belong in the same world.

"I was picking her up so I could take her out for her birthday," Lis continued. "It was a beautiful night and I was early, so I got out of the car and sat on a concrete bench near the entrance. Rudy was there, sitting in a wheelchair waiting for a cab to take him home."

My eyes widened. "After his brakes failed," I said, realizing the timing of that visit.

Lis nodded. "He was a very different Rudy from the one I was used to when he played Santa."

"Different how?" Arno asked.

She shrugged, falling silent as Max returned.

The waitress handed Arno his coffee. "Sorry that took so long, hon. That old coffee maker is on its last legs, I'm afraid. I'm going to have to get a new one." She made the statement as if she was talking about burying her beloved pet.

She might as well bury the thing. I'd tasted the coffee the elderly machine made. I was pretty sure it was already spitting out dirt.

I wisely kept my opinion on her coffee to myself as Max jotted down our orders. As she trotted away, I looked expectantly toward Lis.

"Rudy? Right. He was just, I don't know, so dark and depressed. He was banged up and I was sure he was in some pain. But this seemed deeper than that. It was…" She blinked as something clarified in her mind. "He was mad. Not sad. I realize, looking back that the emotion I took as sadness was really more like rage. He kept saying, 'someone did this to me'."

"Did he say who?"

"No, just that it wasn't an accident."

"I watched him leave in that cab and couldn't

help wondering what he'd done to make someone so angry he suspected they'd tamper with his brakes to get back at him."

"Joey and I talked to the guy who did his brakes," Hal said. "Supposedly, he was a friend of Rudy's from way back."

"The mechanic in Ormsville?" Arno asked.

Hal nodded.

"I think I'll drive over there tomorrow and have a chat with him."

"I still don't understand why Rudy didn't bring the truck to the Greasy Wrench," I said. "I didn't really get the impression from Mike that they were that close. And brakes aren't his main business. If a mistake was made…"

"It seems likely Mike's Mechanics made it?" Hal said, nodding. "I agree."

"It might be easier to understand than you think," Arno offered.

We all looked his way expectantly. He took a sip of his dirt coffee and winced, picking something from his teeth. Probably a small rock or a mouse bone from the dirt. "Someone he apparently didn't like very much works at the Greasy Wrench."

"Who?" we all asked in unison before laughing.

"Lynn Dwyer."

Hal and I shared a look.

"Well, I guess we know where we need to go tomorrow," Hal said.

I nodded.

"Okay, that's enough doom and gloom," Lis said as Max approached with our plates.

We all agreed she was right and settled in to enjoy our chicken and noodles over mashed potatoes.

Also known as "carb on carb crime".

CHAPTER 9

My cell rang as we headed across Deer Hollow to speak to the mechanic at The Greasy Wrench. I looked at the ID. "It's Madge," I told Arno.

"Hey, Madge."

"Joey. I'm glad I caught you. I'm getting ready to leave the office and I won't be back for a few days. I wanted to let you know that I bit the bullet and went through those files today. I found some old records on a Pete Landscoff offer. You were right. He did work with the previous owner of this office."

"He made another unsolicited offer to Rudy?"

"Worse. He tried to buy the place when Rudy was buying it. He apparently offered the current owner several thousand dollars over asking price, but Rudy won the bid anyway. To say that Landscoff was mad about it would be a giant understatement. I guess he threatened the Agent."

I glanced at Arno. "Threatened her? How?"

"He told her he'd bury her. That she'd never succeed in Deer Hollow. And then I guess he made harassing phone calls to her nearly every day for a month afterward. Real psychotic stuff. I'm starting to think that poor woman sold this business because of Landscoff more than anything else."

"That surprises me. Landscoff doesn't seem like that kind of guy." I thought about it for a moment. "Was there anything in the original sale file about Lynn Dwyer's supposed proof that the property line was wrong?"

"Actually, there was. Dwyer was wrong. The document that she's claiming is a survey was actually just an old property line drawing the original owner of her plot had drawn up. It wasn't official and wasn't based on any accurate measurements of the property. They apparently went by concrete markers and just guessed at the boundary lines. Rudy had a survey drawn when he bought the house. Those trees were on his property."

"Can you mail me those records?" I asked Madge.

"Sure thing. You have a nice holiday, Joey."

"You too. Thanks so much for digging that information up." I disconnected and told Hal what I'd learned.

He listened intently. "It sounds like Landscoff requires a closer look."

"Yeah," I agreed. "Maybe we can drop by his house after we have this interview."

* * *

The Greasy Wrench was located on one of the short spokes of road jutting off either side of Main Street in Deer Hollow. The offshoots were like angry outbursts of asphalt and gravel, sporting an ugly array of businesses, interspersed with the occasional home or double-wide trailer.

The street, called Skunk Stripe Road, probably because of the too-wide stripe painted down its center by what was apparently a drunk with dimensional issues, was home to the repair shop as well as a tattoo parlor, a vape store, and a tiny home that housed the town's local seamstress.

The Wrench sat at the very end of the dead-end street and took up most of the short road, its skeletal metal victims, in various states of death, were draped over every available piece of gravel and blade of grass along its property.

I didn't envy the seamstress and the other businesses for the view they looked at on a daily basis.

Hal and I parked in the only open spot we could find amid the jumble of cars and their parts and walked inside. I shivered violently as the door closed behind us, glad to be out of the icy wind. It had started to snow again as we headed out, and the forecast had it snowing for the next twenty-four hours.

At least Santa and the kids should be happy. There'd definitely be snow on Christmas morning.

"Hello?" Hal's voice got lost amid the greasy, disemboweled contents of the shop, really little more than a repurposed gas station from the days when they were called service stations and actually provided services other than pumping gas and selling expensive groceries.

There was no bright, clean mini-mart at the Greasy Wrench. But there was a whole lot of the stuff indicated by its name.

A.k.a. grease.

"Be right there," someone said. The voice was distorted, as if the speaker was holding something in his mouth when he talked. A thick pair of legs stuck out from under the truck at the center of the shop. The oversized tires probably made it easier for the mechanic, whose lower half promised a beefy kind of guy, to slide underneath it on one of those rolling things.

The heels of a pair of big, black boots kicked against a concrete floor that had once been painted an ugly gray and was currently painted an even uglier grease. A thick form rolled out from underneath the massive vehicle.

The woman was probably five feet nine and weighed well over two hundred pounds if I had to guess. Her oversized head was made larger by a wild nest of curly brown hair that I suspected came from the inside of a perm bottle. Some of the nest was flattened around the top by a stained and tatty bandana tied in a firm knot in back.

Lynn Dwyer narrowed her gaze on me. "I know you."

I nodded, my hand twitching upward before I realized I didn't want to shake hers. It was black with grease that she was wiping down the front of her coveralls. "You held a shotgun on me yesterday."

She laughed. "That's right. And here you are again. You're a persistent little thing, aren't ya?"

I jerked my head toward Hal. "I brought muscle this time."

She laughed again, her brown eyes sparkling with good humor. Quite a different reaction than I'd gotten standing in the snowdrift of her front yard. "He's a good-lookin' guy. But I'm kind of partial to the cute little blonde muscle you had with you last time."

I couldn't help smiling. "Yeah, she's kind of a fan favorite."

Silence carried the next couple of beats, and Hal shifted forward. "Hal Amity." He bravely shook her hand. "Ms. Fulle and I are helping the Sheriff's office run down some of the details surrounding Rudy Hortmann's death."

"That's what she told me." Lynn shook her head. "I'm not sure what y'all think I can tell you, but I'm happy ta help if I can."

"I understand he had his truck towed here after the accident?"

She nodded. "He wanted me ta tell 'im the brakes was tampered with. I couldn't do that."

"You're sure they weren't?"

"I'm sure they wasn't cut. I *did* find grease on the brake pads. If they was greased, that could cause failure. But it would be hard to control how or when that would happen. More likely oil dripped onto the pads after the crash."

Hal nodded. "Was that the first time Rudolf Hortmann brought his truck into this shop?"

She shrugged. "I haven't seen him here before or since. But I'm not always here. You can ask the owner."

"Ms. Dwyer," I said, "did you by any chance call Deer Hollow Realtor the other day, to ask about the value of Rudy Hortmann's property?"

She narrowed a hostile gaze on me. "You think I sized up his worth before I killed him?"

I shrugged. It was harsh, but that was basically what I was asking.

She chuckled darkly. "Do I look stupid to you?"

I refused to answer that on the grounds it might

earn me a wrench to the head. "Madge at Deer Hollow Realtor got a phone call the morning of Rudy's death from a woman who wanted to know the value of the property. I know you've shown some interest in the property, so I thought I'd ask."

"No. I didn't call no realtor. My only interest in that property is the part where it bleeds onto mine."

I wisely refrained from correcting her misinformation. I figured the next owner of that property would be dealing with the issue. Probably legally. I wished them well.

Hal handed her a card. "Thanks for your help. If you think of anything else…"

She held up the card, nodding. "I'll give ya a call."

I felt her stare burrowing between my shoulder blades as we left. It was almost a relief to step out into the bright sun, despite the icy wind pummeling us as we hurried back to Hal's car. As soon as we were closed inside and the heat was going, I turned to Hal. "Do you believe her?"

"About the brakes?" He nodded. "Yeah. She's right. There's no way someone who wants to sabotage a car could grease up some brake pads to do it. Rudy would most likely have crashed before he got out of the lot."

"Why do I sense a 'but' in there?"

"I'm not sure. Something about her just doesn't ring true. I couldn't help feeling like she was lying to us about something."

"Maybe she had a bigger disagreement with Rudy and doesn't want us to find out."

Hal put the car into gear. "I'm sure it's something like that."

His cell rang and he looked at the ID. "It's Arno." He put the car back into *Park* and answered on speaker. "Hey, Arno. You have both of us."

"I finally got a call back from the Detective in charge of the Tannie Bishopson murder. He told me he pulled Rudy into interview. Apparently, somebody caught him on video talking to the victim the day before she was killed. The conversation looked pretty heated."

"Yet he didn't charge him. Why not?"

"No proof at all he did anything but talk to her. But the girl's family was livid. Most of them left the area after a year, claiming Tannie's killer was never going to be found because the police were inept. As you can imagine, that was a sore spot for the detective."

"I'll bet," Hal said, grimacing.

I wondered if he'd ever been in a similar situation when he'd been an Indianapolis detective.

"Public opinion went against Rudy?" Hal asked.

"Local papers printed a story about his disease. The police spoke to his doctor, and he insisted Rudy's bipolar disease was mild and easily controlled with his meds. There was no indication at all that he'd stopped taking them. Despite all the possibilities Rudy offered on the case, they had nothing they could hold him with."

"I'll bet they'd have loved to have found that gun back then," I said. For the first time, I was seriously considering whether Rudy actually *had* killed that girl.

"No doubt," Arno agreed. "The detective actually said he took a look at Rudy's friend, Mike Palmer but they had no prior relationship between Palmer and the girl, no physical evidence, and no witnesses to put him at the scene either. They had nothing. I'm going to take another look at Palmer. He does fit the vague physical description the police got at the time. It would be nice to give that girl's family some closure and solve our own case at the same time."

"I think we'll go back to Rudy's," Hal said, glancing at me. "We can stop by Landscoff's place while we're there."

I nodded.

"Landscoff?" Arno asked. "Do you have new information on him?"

I told Arno about what Madge discovered about Landscoff's aggressive interest in Rudy's property.

"Okay, let me know what you find." Arno hesitated. "The ME's office got back to me on the results of Rudy's autopsy."

"That was fast," Hal said. "Especially for this time of year."

"Yeah, it was pretty straight forward. Toxicology

came back clean. No surprise that strangulation was the cause of death, but there is one interesting thing. He was probably out cold when he was strangled."

"But you said tox was negative," Hal said, sliding me a look.

"It was. He was knocked out. ME's thinking the killer used a torque wrench, judging by the shape of the wound."

"Defensive wounds?" I asked.

"None. Either the killer snuck up on him in the snow and wind, or he it was somebody he knew and trusted."

* * *

*W*e decided to speak to Landscoff first, and then revisit Rudy's. As we turned down his freshly plowed drive, I noticed the lid on Landscoff's trash can had blown back and several boxes stuffed into the top seemed about to blow out.

One of the boxes caught my eye. I remembered seeing one like it in Rudy's kitchen trash can. The box was decorated with oversized, multi-colored bulbs stretched across a white background with evergreen trees dotting the background.

Interesting that they used the same brand of Christmas lights. But not necessarily a smoking gun. The small hardware store in Deer Hollow only sold a couple of brands.

Hal parked in front of a sprawling ranch home, with grayed-cedar siding and large windows that overlooked the picturesque lawn.

We stepped out of the car and looked around. The place had a totally different feel from Rudy's, and I couldn't help wondering why Landscoff had wanted Rudy's place so badly.

Pete Landscoff answered his door almost immediately as if he'd been waiting for us to arrive. His plain face held a pleasant expression that gave away nothing. If he was surprised to see us, he certainly didn't show it. "Hello. What a pleasant surprise. Do you have more questions about Rudy?"

Landscoff addressed me because we'd already met. But his gaze slid toward Hal as he extended his hand.

Hal shook it. "Mr. Landscoff. I'm Hal Amity. I'm sure Ms. Fulle told you we're helping the Sheriff with some legwork on the Hortmann case."

Landscoff nodded. "She did. Would you like to come in?"

"Thank you, that would be nice," I said.

We followed him inside and Landscoff closed the door behind us, locking both the handle and the deadbolt before turning back to us.

He must have noticed my curious expression because he laughed softly. "Habit. I lived in a slightly dicey part of Indianapolis for years. I'm afraid I got used to locking the door whenever I was in the house, no matter what time of day."

I gave him a smile. "I can appreciate that. Even in the country, trouble still manages to rear its ugly head."

"Yes." He rubbed his hands together, his tall body slightly hunched and his manner a bit jittery. "Can I get you coffee? Or a glass of water?"

"No. Thanks," Hal said. "If we could just ask you a couple of questions?"

Landscoff inclined his head. "Of course." He indicated two long couches in the room off the entrance. "Shall we sit?"

We stepped down from the slate-tiled entryway onto cream-colored carpet and sat down on a mustard yellow couch. Landscoff sat down across from us on a matching couch. He sat forward, resting his elbows on his skinny legs, and waited with an air of expectation.

"This is a beautiful place," Hal said, seeming to catch Landscoff by surprise.

"It is, isn't it? I'm very happy here. I built it myself." He laughed self-deprecatingly. "Well, I designed it and had it built. I'm pretty worthless with tools."

I couldn't help wondering if he was giving us a little jab. A sinister inside joke, given that Rudy had been hit with a wrench. "It's beautiful," I agreed. "But it's so different from Rudy's place. I was wondering why you made so many offers on his property when you have this wonderful spot?"

Landscoff nodded as if he'd been expecting my question. "I actually built this house after my initial attempts to buy the place next door didn't pan out. I'm actually much happier here. I would have had to do major renovations to that cabin to make it feel like home."

"Yet you've made several additional offers over the last two years," Hal said. "Why?"

"I actually wanted the land more than the house. I'd like more property. And I'd planned on expanding the tree farm. I love the idea of growing trees."

"You worked with Deer Hollow Realtors?" I asked, watching for his reaction. I wasn't disappointed.

Landscoff's lips curled as if he'd tasted something foul. "Unfortunately. Terrible agents. They have no imagination at all. I'm afraid I got rather angry with them when I lost the house. I'm guessing, from your questions that you already knew that."

"Their records indicate that you threatened the agent with violence and then harassed her," Hal told the man. "You can probably understand why we'd find that interesting, given Rudy Hortmann's murder."

Landscoff sighed. "Look, Mr. Amity. I didn't kill Rudy. Yeah, I'll admit I wanted his property. I'll even admit I was an ass about it back then. But I was lucky enough to get this property and I love it. I'm very happy and, as I told Ms. Fulle before, Rudy and I got along just fine. I held no grudges against him."

I wasn't sure if I believed him or not. But there was one further thing I needed to clarify. "I noticed you have no Christmas decorations, Mr. Landscoff. You don't celebrate?"

He shook his head, frowning. "My memories of the season aren't wonderful. I find no joy in it. And, since I live here by myself, I have no need to rise above my dislike of the holiday and pretend otherwise."

"I'm sorry to hear that," I told him. "I did notice you had an empty box for Christmas lights in your trash."

Landscoff frowned thoughtfully. After a beat, he nodded. "Yes. That blew over from Rudy's yard. Probably from when he strung the lights around that tree near the road."

Hal stood up, handing Landscoff his card. "I'd appreciate it if you'd stay available, in case we have any further questions."

Landscoff nodded. And if he seemed a little more eager to usher us *out* of his house, than he'd been to usher us into it, I tried not to hold it against him.

After all, he wasn't imbued by the Christmas spirit.

And that made me wonder if he might have

embraced his inner Grinch. And throttled the man who'd kept him from getting what he wanted.

* * *

*D*espite the bitter cold, we decided to start in the detached garage. The chances of the wrench used to incapacitate Rudy being in his own garage were slim, but you could never predict how a killer's mind was going to work.

Built from the same, light-colored logs as the house, the building was big enough for one car, or truck, and deep enough to park Rudy's riding lawn mower at the back.

Unlike the commercial garages we'd recently visited, Rudy's garage was clean and smelled like fresh lumber. His tools were carefully organized in a large, rubberized cabinet and on a pegboard with a variety of hangers to keep the tools visible and tidy.

Below the corkboard was a wood-topped work-bench. On that bench was a shiny, red metal toolbox.

The rubberized cabinet had a series of drawers that someone had marked with their contents. Hal was searching those drawers for wrenches, so I took the toolbox. Inside the box was a massive jumble of old bolts and screws, bent rusted nails, short coils of wire in a variety of lengths and sizes, and the most common tools, which included screwdrivers in a variety of sizes and heads, a couple of wrenches, none of which were torque wrenches the way Hal described them to me, an old hammer and some other stuff I couldn't identify.

An hour later, we'd both come up empty, except for a smear of dirty grease on the inside of the small door.

Hal took a picture of the smear and the location and sent it to Arno. Outside the building, we found a set of wobbly tracks in the snow. They led to the tree farm and then veered off toward Lynn's place, stopping about twenty yards from her house.

"Did she fly from here?" I walked a bit farther, trying to see if someone had smoothed the tracks out. It was impossible to tell. Though there were signs that a wide strip of about five yards was a wind zone. There were drifts and wind-tracks in the snow to prove it. Once I got closer to the house, there were too many tracks to trace.

There were even a few pawprints leftover from the day before.

Hal was frowning down at the tracks. "Those were made with big boots."

"Like the ones Lynn was wearing at work today?" I pointed out helpfully.

He kept frowning.

"What's wrong?"

He finally glanced up at me. "What?"

"You're frowning at those tracks."

"Oh. It's nothing. They just look off to me some-how. I was trying to figure out why."

"They look like about the right size to be Lynn's," I said.

"Yeah, they definitely do. I'd say they were made last night or this morning." He started walking back toward the house.

"Why would Lynn go over to Rudy's? Especially his garage?"

"Simple curiosity? If she thinks she's going to buy the place, she'd want to check it out."

"And a woman like Lynn would probably start by checking out the garage," I said. Hal was right. We were probably just tracking an excited home buyer.

A pair of birds swooped low in front of me and I jolted to a surprised stop. "These birds are having a good time." I watched them swoop from tree to tree, occasionally landing on top of the snow and pecking at it as if looking for the ground.

My gaze caught on a spot of color in the snow. I reached out to stop Hal. "Hold up, what's that?"

We moved closer to see what was lying in the snow. Hal threw out an arm to stop me a couple of yards away. "Hold up."

"What is it?" I asked, trying to get taller so I could see it from his much higher perspective.

Hal tugged out his cell phone. "If my suspicion is right, it's our murder weapon."

CHAPTER 10

*A*rno dropped the wrench into a paper evidence bag and glanced our way. "There's hair and blood on this. I'd say there's a better than average chance it was from our killer." He handed the bag to a deputy and walked over to the area beyond the crime scene tape where Hal and I waited.

"We'll try to get prints off of it but I'm guessing we won't have any luck. In this weather, the killer will have been wearing gloves."

"Maybe there'll be an old one," Hal offered.

Arno nodded, his gaze sliding to Lynn Dwyer's place. "I'm getting a warrant to search Lynn's place. My guess is we'll find the boots she was wearing when she killed him. If we're lucky, there'll be blood on them."

Hal stared at the tracks. He was frowning again.

What was it about those tracks? I let my gaze

slide to the boot prints in the snow. After a moment, it hit me. "They aren't deep enough."

Hal's gaze slid to mine and he gave me a slow smile. "Good job, partner."

"What are you two talking about?" Arno asked.

Hal pointed to the trail of prints. "How much would you say the wearer of those boots weighs?"

Arno walked over and crouched down a few feet away. "Hard to tell in these conditions. With ice or hard-pack snow, weight can be hard to determine."

"There's no ice and the snow isn't hard pack here," Hal said.

Arno stuck a finger into the snow, frowning. He stood up and shook his head.

"Lynn Dwyer's not a small woman," I said. "She's maybe, what? Two hundred pounds?"

"Probably more like two-fifty," Arno agreed. "She's more muscle than fat."

"So why are her prints so shallow?" Hal asked.

"We got a quarter of an inch of snow last night," Arno reminded him. "That's probably skewing the prints."

Hal nodded but didn't look completely convinced.

My cell rang and I looked at it. The ID was for Deer Hollow Veterinary Office. I answered on the third ring, my gloves hampering me. "Hello?"

"Joey?"

I recognized the gruff, creaky voice. "Hey, Doc."

"I promised you the information on that pig."

Just the mention of Ethel made me grin. "Yes. Did you find something?"

"I have my original notes. Rudy got the pig from a friend of his. Appears she was a Christmas gift to the friend's daughter. When she started getting bigger, the kid lost interest. Rudy pretty much rescued that pig from what sounded like a situation that was at the very least neglectful and, at worst, slightly abusive."

My heart broke. I sent Hal a look that had him coming over to put an arm around me. "Poor Ethel."

Doc grunted out an agreement. "Yeah, I gave him a fifty percent discount on her initial appointment for rescuing her."

I knew there was a reason I loved Doc Beetle. "Rudy didn't by any chance tell you who the friend was, did he?"

"No. But he did say it was somebody in Ormsville."

That place just kept popping up. "Okay, thanks, Doc."

"There's just one more thing. The pig was traumatized when Rudy got her. He bought her a stuffed frog to help her cope. You might want to see if you can find it for her now. It might help her get through the next few weeks."

"Good idea. I'll do that."

I disconnected with Doc and looked at Hal. "We need to go back to Rudy's."

"What's wrong?"

I sniffled, swiping at the tears sliding down my cheeks. "I'll fill you in on the way."

* * *

*H*al's face was grim as we searched the small house for the stuffed frog. His jaw had grown more rigid by the moment as I'd told him how Rudy and Ethel had started out. When he saw the look on my face, he pulled me into a hug. "Rudy loved that pig," he told me. "He erased all those bad experiences and gave her a happy life. We're going to make sure that happy life continues."

I nodded. But his words created a new fear in me. We would try to find Ethel a great home, but people weren't always what they seemed. What if we picked badly? I couldn't bear for Ethel to lose Rudy and then go back to a sad and lonely life.

We stood in the center of Rudy's tidy living room, looking around. It was pretty much as it had been when we were there last. The teepee style tent still sat in a quiet corner near the fireplace. The stale scent of an old fire competed with the fresh pine scent of the tree Rudy had placed in front of the window. Covered in cute pig ornaments and over-sized, multi-colored lights, the little Christmas tree managed to still look festive. I grinned at the strand of popcorn that was mostly just string in the spots Ethel could reach.

There was one small, brightly wrapped package sitting on the red velvet and white fake fur tree skirt. I walked over to look at the package and saw Ethel's name scrawled across the Christmas pig sticker on front. I reached for the package. "Do you think Rudy would mind if I took this and we gave it to her on Christmas?"

Hal smiled. "I think he'd like that."

I nodded, hugging the package to my belly as another wave of sadness filled me.

"Let's find that frog and get home," Hal urged. "I don't like to leave her alone for too long."

We split up and he took the bedrooms while I searched the kitchen and living room. Hal came back a few minutes later, empty-handed. I'd searched everywhere but the teepee. Dropping to my knees, I tugged one side of the door flaps open and stuck my head inside. There, amid a jumble of soft, fleece blankets in a dainty pink color, I found the frog.

I emerged with it, grinning. "This must have been her hidey-hole."

Hal nodded. "I read that pigs need a spot to go for downtime."

The frog body was big, about eighteen inches across, circular, with long skinny arms and legs. Its belly was slightly crusty as if a cute little pink snout had snorfled it a few hundred times. I looked back at the blankets. "I wonder if we should take these too."

Hal nodded. "They'd probably make her feel more comfortable."

I tugged one out and threw it to Hal, grabbing the second one and exclaiming in surprise as a bunch of stuff fell out of it. "What about the tent?"

"No, let's leave it intact for now. Arno might not appreciate our removing it before the investigation is closed," he said.

I crawled halfway inside to examine the treasure trove, which consisted of a hairbrush, a toothbrush, a few flashcards like someone would buy for toddlers, a half-eaten apple and a woman's earring.

I grabbed the earring and pulled it out, holding it up for Hal to see. It was a large, antiqued silver cross, and it looked as if it might be expensive. "I wonder whose this is?"

Hal frowned. "Did Rudy have a girlfriend?" He took a picture of the earing and I placed it back into the tent.

"Not that I know of, but maybe we can ask Arno that. He might know."

Hal grabbed the second blanket and shook it out, quickly folding it to match the first one. "You ready?"

I threw the apple into the trash and we left after making sure everything was as we'd found it. Then we headed home to check on all our fur babies. I was anxious to get home anyway. I had something in mind for the evening that I hoped would make their Christmas extra special.

* * *

*I*n the end, I'd have to say the popcorn stringing was a success. But it wasn't pretty.

Caphy definitely ate more of the popcorn than eventually got strung up. She kept stealing it from the bowl before I got a chance to sew it onto the string.

I'd have to give her props though, she was very sneaky. Half the time, I only knew she'd been in there when I picked up a handful of soggy kernels.

She lay beside the couch, looking innocent. Which was how I knew without a doubt she was guilty.

Ethel probably ate as much as Caphy, but she preferred her popcorn already strung up. The end result was that, by the time I finally gave up, I had a very sparse strand about four feet long that I simply draped across the front of the tree.

Hal grinned at the paltry results of my efforts. "Very...um...pretty?"

"Stop talking," I told him, scrubbing the back of my hand over my sweaty brow. "Note to self. Never try to string popcorn with a dog, a pig, and a cat in the room."

Hal skimmed a look toward LaLee, who was batting two pieces of popcorn around the room as if they were the best thing since catnip.

He kissed my temple. "It's perfect. And you got the desired result, right? You wanted the animals to enjoy the experience."

And enjoy it they had. I nodded. "I guess I had delusions of grandeur. I'd thought I'd wrap the whole tree in popcorn strands."

I gathered up the bowl and my stringing tools and headed toward the kitchen. Ethel ran along with me but diverged once inside the big room and dove under the tent Hal had made for her by throwing a large comforter over three of my kitchen chairs. We'd arranged the blankets from Rudy's inside the makeshift tent and thrown her stuffed frog on top of them.

Hal grinned when he saw her snatch the frog up and toss her head, flinging it around like Caphy liked to fling her stuffed babies. "I swear she's part dog."

I joined him in a grin. "Except she listens better."

"There is that."

Ethel released the frog and flopped down on her blankets, dropping her heavy head onto the toy like a pillow.

It crunched.

Hal and I shared a look.

I frowned. "What was that?"

He shook his head. Walking over to the tent, Hal replaced the frog with one of the pillows we'd thrown inside the tent and carried it over to the counter. He pressed against the toy's round body and it crunched again. "That sounds like paper," I told him.

He ran his fingers over the terry-cloth-like surface. "Several papers, if I'm not wrong. Tri-folded like a letter."

I dug in my junk drawer and came up with a pair of scissors, handing them to Hal.

"We're going to cut up her frog?"

"Just one slice. I'll repair it," I promised.

It turned out there was already a repaired cut in the toy. Hal just clipped the stitches in that and reached into the fiberfill stuffing. He pulled out a stack of notebook paper, folded to fit into a letter-sized envelope. The handwriting on the pages was large and sprawling, but it was fairly legible despite that. The notes appeared to have been written in black ink.

"What is it?" I asked Hal.

He scanned the first page and then glanced up at me, surprise clear on his face. "These are notes about the coed's murder. It looks like Rudy was investigating it."

CHAPTER 11

"Rudy must have known he was in danger," I told Hal and Arno. "For him to hide those records in Ethel's toy."

Arno scratched Caphy behind the ears as he read through the notes we'd found. When he looked up, he seemed perplexed.

"What do you make of all that?" Hal asked the cop.

"Clearly, Rudy had some idea who killed the girl and was looking for proof."

I nodded. "I wish he'd written the identity down," I told the men. "Because I'm betting that person killed him."

"That would be a good guess," Arno said. Shaking his head, he sat back in the chair and watched me sew the frog back together. "At least we have Rudy's version of why he'd been spotted talking to Tannie

Bishopson."

Rudy had written that he'd tried to warn the girl about the person he believed eventually killed her.

"He talked like he knew the person," Hal offered. "He implied the person had all the signs of having a troubled mind."

"What does that even mean?" I asked, frowning.

"Usually it means they've shown signs of anti-social or sociopathic behavior. Things like threatening to shoot up a place, or physically harming people or animals."

I thought about that, recalling Doc's information about Ethel Squeaks. "Doc Beetle said Rudy rescued Ethel from someone who'd been neglectful or abusive. I wonder if that could be the same person?"

"If not," Arno said, "That's an awful big coincidence."

"And coincidence doesn't make for good investigations," I said, nodding. "This person lived in Ormsville," I told the two men. "I think maybe it's time to revisit Mike's Mechanics."

* * *

*I*n the end, Arno left us to talk to the mechanic. He got a call about a multi-vehicle pile-up on the highway, and it was "all hands on deck" for the Sherriff's department.

It had started to snow as we left the house. The

winding, hilly roads leading to Ormsville were treacherous in the conditions, and Hal drove slowly. More than once, we found ourselves caught behind a snowplow going even slower than Hal had been going.

Still, the beautiful but deadly views of plunging ravines and snow-covered trees on either side of the twisty road removed any impatience I might have felt to get to our destination.

As it was, my mind was churning with all the stuff I still needed to do before the morning. Which would be Christmas.

* * *

Twenty nerve-wracking minutes later, Hal turned off the slick main road onto the gravel country road that fed Mike's. A minute later, we entered the small lot. I noticed that several of the vehicles and machines which had been parked there the last time we visited were gone. The lot was empty except for a red pickup with the words, Mike's Mechanics and a phone number on the side, and a gold sedan with a rusty dent on the passenger side door.

I wondered if Mike was working on the car. I noted the black gloss beneath the sedan that told me it had an oil leak. That would certainly bolster his claim that he wasn't totally out of the large engine side of the business.

Or, if the car was Mike's, it might put him at the scene of Rudy's murder.

The door jangled cheerfully as we entered the garage.

Hal called out. Nobody answered. We set out across the building, heading for a large, commercial mower that sat beneath a bright lamp like someone was working on it. A large, rolling toolbox stood near the lamp. As we got close, I saw a greasy towel like the one I'd seen Mike wipe his hands on lying on the dusty concrete. I sucked in a gasp, my hand snapping out to grab Hal's arm. "Hal. Look."

He eyed the greasy towel, his gaze focusing in on the bright spot of red saturating the cloth.

"Is that blood?" I whispered.

He moved closer, reaching for the gun in the small of his back.

We quickly forgot the towel as we rounded the oversized mower and found Mike, face down on the concrete with a bleeding hole in his skull. A huge wrench lay beside him, his fingers curled mere inches away as if he'd been holding it before he died. Blood formed a puddle beneath his greasy, dark head.

Hal crouched next to the mechanic and felt for a pulse. He frowned, looking at me and shaking his head.

My nose caught the pleasing scent of cinnamon, and it spurred a memory.

A chill slipped over me as the recollection flared.

A pale face. Slender fingers worrying a necklace, and a cool recounting of what had to be a traumatic memory. In that moment, the pieces fell together and I knew.

I stepped closer to Hal as he straightened, gun in hand. "I know who killed Mike and Rudy."

Hal's attention slipped past me as if he hadn't heard. His handsome face hardened.

I knew she was there before I turned around.

The icy muzzle of a gun, smelling of cordite and metal, pressed against the base of my skull. "Too bad you had to come snooping around," a feminine voice said. "I really didn't want to kill you."

I took a deep breath, fighting for calm. "Why'd you kill him? He was your father, wasn't he?"

She laughed softly, the sound bereft of humor. "He was a sperm donor. And he was a killer."

I felt the gun move against my skull as I imagined she shrugged. "I guess we have that in common, he and I."

"He killed Tannie, didn't he?" I guessed. "She tried to fight him off and he killed her."

"She was my friend. He was a pig. He always thought women wanted him. And when he figured out they didn't…" She shrugged again.

Hal kept his gaze locked on the girl, his gun

dropping lower. I could see in his face that he didn't want to shoot the young woman. "Why don't you put the gun down and we'll talk," he said. "Nobody else needs to die."

Out of the corner of my eye, I saw her head shaking. "No. I'm not going to jail." She snorted out a harsh laugh. "I guess the sperm donor and I have that in common too."

We needed time to figure out how to subdue the girl without hurting her. So I'd keep her talking. "I don't understand," I told her. "If you killed Rudy because he figured out Mike killed Tannie, you were protecting your father. You must have loved him."

"You got that wrong. I killed him because he was part of it. They made a deal, the two of them. After it was done, Rudy helped the sperm donor cover it up. He might as well have killed her himself."

"He tried to warn Tannie," Hal told her. "That's why he spoke to her that time. To warn her about his friend, Mike."

The girl shook her head again, refusing to believe. After a beat, I felt her attention turn back to me. "I heard what you said. That you knew who killed them. How'd you figure it out?"

I turned my head an inch so I could see her better. "The earring we found at Rudy's house. The cross. It matched the necklace you were wearing when we visited before."

Her hand moved to her chest, covering the cross

she was still wearing. She swore. "I wondered where that earring went. I probably lost it when that stupid pig charged me from that tent. It scared the crap out of me."

"Ethel was your pig once, wasn't she?" I said. "You got her as a Christmas present."

The girl shrugged. "She was cute when she was little. But then she got big and fat, and I didn't think she was cute anymore. I was going to take her to the vet to be put down. But that Rudy guy had a cow. Next thing I knew, he and the sperm donor had agreed that she could go home with him." She shrugged. "No skin off my nose. As long as I didn't have to take care of her anymore."

My heart broke. Ethel had probably recognized the girl at Rudy's and run out to see her. She'd probably been rejected and frightened when the girl screamed at her. In the end, the whole thing had given us the one clue that helped us tie Rudy's murder to the girl. "What were you doing in Rudy's house?"

"I was going to kill him when he came inside. But I didn't want to stay in there with the pig. Pigs can be really mean. I didn't trust her."

"So you waited for Rudy in that little copse of trees by the road?" Hal said. "And when he came home, you snuck up behind him, knocked him on the head with the wrench, and then strangled him with his own Christmas lights."

She smiled, and it made my blood run cold. "I was so smart. I took the wrench from that woman's garage. Borrowed a pair of her giant boots, so that when I made a trail leading to her house and threw the weapon away in those trees, the cops would think she killed him."

It *had* been a pretty smart plan, but not smart enough. In the end, a sweet-natured pig had pointed a hoof right at her. "You called the realtor and asked about the value of the property too, didn't you?"

She grinned. "I knew that woman wanted the place. I figured it would be another nail in her coffin."

I couldn't help wondering what Lynn Dwyer would think about this young girl she didn't even know plotting to frame her for murder. "Did you tamper with Rudy's brakes?"

That made her frown. "So irritating. I should have been done with him then. But he somehow managed to survive it."

"I'm guessing the grease in the garage came from that wrench too?" Hal asked.

"Yeah. Pretty smart, huh?"

"Diabolical," Hal agreed, his expression dark.

The girl jerked the hand holding the gun, snapping it painfully against my skull. "Drop that gun and kick it over to me, or I'll kill her."

Hal barely hesitated a beat, his mouth a tight line. When he'd done as she said, she pointed to the floor beside Mike. "Kneel down there and put your hands flat against the wall."

Hal's gaze found mine. "No. Let Joey go."

"That's not going to happen. You have two choices. Either you die together and fast, or I kill you first and then take my time with her. You'll die knowing she was tortured because of your stubbornness."

His face darkened with anger and a vein pulsed in his muscular throat. "It's okay, Hal," I told him, holding his gaze for a beat before I lowered it to the wrench a few inches away. I prayed he'd get my message.

Hal turned a murderous look on her. "I'm trusting you to keep your word."

The girl didn't respond.

He turned and lowered to his knees, his hands spread wide on the wall. From where his left hand rested, it was a quick swipe of his hand to grab the wrench.

I started to walk over and join him, but the girl grabbed my arm. "Not just yet..."

Lights flashed over the front window. The girl stilled, probably thinking they were from a police car. She turned to look and I knew I wouldn't get a better chance. I dropped to my knees. "Hal!"

He threw himself sideways as I hit the floor. The girl fired wildly, the bullet blasting into the painted concrete block of the wall.

She swung the gun downward, intending to shoot the closest target.

Which would be me.

I scrabbled for Hal's discarded gun, but she kicked out, hitting me on the shoulder. Pain blossomed through my arm, but I ignored it, swinging my hand upward and hitting her wrist.

She fired again.

The impact of my strike sent the next bullet into the floor a foot away from me.

With a yelp, I hit the floor as something heavy flew over my head and hit the girl in the center of the chest.

She grunted in pain, and a large body rushed past me, driving her to the ground.

Hal hauled her over and tugged the girl's hands behind her back as she bellowed in frustration and pain.

"Call Arno," he instructed me. I dropped to my butt, panting wildly, and dialed Arno's number. Then I leaned back against the wall, watching as Hal snapped an oversized zip tie he'd apparently pulled from the big rolling tool chest around her wrists.

Hal sat back on his heels and looked at me. "You okay?"

I nodded, still panting from fear and exertion. "You?"

"Nothing that won't heal." That was when I noticed the blood on his forehead. "Your head."

He touched it, looking at the blood on his fingers as if it were a spot of grease. "Ricochet from the wall. It's just a scratch."

I decided to take him at his word for the moment. I'd take a look at it when we got home. "Well, this could have gone better."

Hal smiled. "Not really. We caught a murderer, solved an old murder case, and helped Arno close the current case, and there's still time to hit the mall and finish up our shopping."

I groaned, my chin dropping to my chest. "You really know how to hurt a girl."

$\mathcal{I}$ stood in front of the living room window, staring out at the thick curtain of snowflakes drifting down. I was stuck in that in-between place I always went to on Christmas morning since my parents were declared dead, though I'd recently learned my mom was still alive. I was caught between my happy childhood memories of the big house and Christmas mornings with my parents, and happy anticipation of future Christmas memories built with friends and loved ones I still had.

Even if they couldn't be with me to celebrate.

The thought made me sad. I wondered what my mother and Uncle Dev were doing right at that moment.

Probably sleeping.

It was only five o'clock in the morning, and most

normal adults were still happily snoring under a warm mountain of covers.

I'd never been able to sleep in at Christmas. I doubted I ever would. It had always been a magical time for me. A time filled with love and light, promise, and expectation.

Speaking of love…

My thoughts turned to Hal and I smiled. Despite the rough beginning to our evening, Hal had managed to make our late-night excursion into last-minute Christmas shopping fun and memorable.

By the time the local cops and Arno had let us leave the scene, everything had mostly been closed. It was close to Midnight and all we could find was a large discount store a few miles from Ormsville.

We'd made it work. And, coupled with planned Christmas day visits to all my friends to give them cookies and sing Christmas carols badly and off-key, I knew the presents we'd found would be perfect.

They couldn't be anything else. Because they'd been selected with love and would be given wrapped in the same sentiment.

I smelled the rich scent of coffee before I heard his footsteps on the wood floor. I smiled as a strong arm wrapped around me from behind, holding a steaming cup of coffee. "Mm, my hero."

He chuckled softly. "I didn't see that turkey in the oven yet."

I sighed. "I needed a minute just to enjoy the season."

His chin found the top of my head. We watched the falling snow in silence for a moment, Hal's enormous heart pounding against my back.

"It's beautiful," he finally said. "Even if I am starting to worry we won't get out of here until spring."

"Would that be so bad?"

"Well, we do have turkey and cookies."

I laughed. "And a pibl."

I could almost feel him frown. "There is that. We're going to need more food."

Said pibl's nails clicked over the hardwood floor of the living room. Her wide, warm tongue bathed the back of my calf in greeting. I looked down. "Hey, pretty girl."

Soft grunting followed. We turned to find Ethel trotting toward us from the kitchen with her frog in her mouth. "Hey, sleepyhead," I said, grinning.

"All we need is the cat and we can open presents."

"We should probably start the turkey first."

"It can wait." He grinned. "I don't think you can."

Heat filled my face. "Am I that obvious?"

"Only to me." Hal kissed me on the nose, taking my nearly empty cup of coffee from me. "I'll get us a refill. You find the cat."

* * *

*a*n hour later, we sat surrounded by torn paper and boxes. I'd wrapped myself in an exquisitely soft new cashmere sweater from Hal, and he was having fun with the dry fire laser toy I'd gotten him so he could practice shooting without going to a range.

The pibl had a pile of new stuffed toys and chewies gathered at her feet, and she was begging me for another nut from the tray of fruit and nuts I'd placed on the table in front of the couch.

Ethel had been happily rolling her new ball around since she opened her own package, and I still held her package from Rudy in my lap, waiting until she lost interest in the ball to give it to her.

LaLee had escaped upstairs with her new catnip mouse so Caphy couldn't get hold of it.

I had a mimosa in my hand and was staring into the fire as Rudolph the Red-Nosed Reindeer played in the background.

It was a perfect moment. Especially when LaLee came back down the stairs and jumped up next to me, curling up beside my hip and purring loudly.

Hal's arm was around my shoulders, but I noticed he kept looking at his watch. I finally had to ask. "Are you worried about the turkey?"

He shook his head. "No, but we should probably get it in soon, or we won't have anything to feed our guests later."

"Guests? What guests?"

Ethel wandered over, snorfling happily.

"Oh, look, she's ready for her last gift," Hal said with a secret smile.

I arched an eyebrow at him. "This discussion isn't over."

He shook his head.

I held the gift out to the pig and her snout quivered, her curly tail spinning with interest. "This is from Rudy," I told her. Tears filled my eyes. "He loved you very much."

Ethel's small eyes lifted to mine. Her ears twitched. She bumped my leg affectionately with her snout.

I sniffled. "Yes, we love you too." I gave her an impulsive kiss between her ears. "Let's see what he got you." I tore the paper off the package and opened the unmarked box, holding it out for her to dig into the tissue paper in search of her gift.

For a moment, I thought she was going to get stuck on the frothy pink tissue and forget about the gift inside.

But she dug her snout deep into the paper and came out with a tiny stuffed toy.

"It's a pig," I said, grinning. The tiny toy had a big red heart sewn onto its chest and a happy smile on its adorable face. "It looks just like you," I told the pig.

She snorted softly and turned around, trotting quickly toward her nest in the kitchen.

"She took it to her tent," Hal said. "It's a new favorite."

I nodded. "Rudy knew her well."

Fresh tears bathed my cheeks. Hal hugged me close. "She's okay, honey. She's going to have a wonderful life."

I nodded, sniffling.

The doorbell rang and Hal jumped to his feet. "Here's your last present." He grabbed my hand, pulling me to my feet.

I scrubbed at my wet cheeks. "What in the world...?"

Hal tucked my hand under his and led me to the front door. "You'll see in a minute."

Caphy shot past me and jumped up on the door, warbling with excitement.

My pulse picked up, my own excitement growing. I couldn't imagine what Hal had done...

He opened the door and I went perfectly still. Too shocked to move.

"Merry Christmas, baby girl."

I squealed and threw myself into my mother's arms. "It's really you! How in the world did you get here through all this snow?"

She laughed, shivering. "We caught a ride in Santa's sleigh." I held her at arm's length, taking in the dense fall of blonde hair curling around her face, the strands of gray a bit more noticeable than the last time I'd seen her. She was wearing a long, red wool coat and black leather boots. Her beautiful face was pink from the cold. She looked wonderful.

Then her words sunk in and I blinked. "We?"

Another form emerged from the snow. A tall one, clean-shaven and handsome. The man's dark brown gaze found mine and held, filled with a plea for forgiveness and understanding. Devon Little had been a friend of my family for as long as I could remember. He was my godfather, and I'd always called him Uncle Dev. I'd recently learned he might have done some things that skirted the law to protect my mom from a ruthless, gangster-like businessman who still pursued her.

I'd been angry more than happy to see him lately. But, in the end, I couldn't fault him for trying to protect his best friend's wife and daughter.

I stepped forward and opened my arms, falling into the familiar hug of a man who'd been like a second father to me for most of my life. "I'm glad you're here."

His hug was nearly painful. "Me too, Joey."

"Let's close this door before the animals get out," Hal said, urging Uncle Dev to take a step into the house.

"Animals? Plural?" Dev asked.

"I have so much to tell you," I said, my eyes moist.

"You can do that while we're fixing the turkey," Hal said, grinning.

My mom's eyes lit up. "Joey and I in the kitchen together, scary and delightful." She waved a hand at Hal and Dev. "You two go watch football or something. We girls have got this."

"It's seven o'clock in the morning," Dev complained.

Hal pounded him on the back. "Come on, I'll let you play with my new toy."

I grabbed Hal before he escaped into the living room with Dev. Standing on my tippy toes, I planted a long, lingering kiss on his yummy lips. When I broke the kiss, he rested his forehead against mine and stayed in my embrace.

"Not that I'm complaining, but what was that for?"

"For giving me the best Christmas present ever. And for being so completely wonderful."

He drew back, his hands coming up to frame my face as he fixed his emerald-green gaze on mine. "I'm the man you inspire me to be, Joey Fulle. And I love you very much."

My eyes started leaking again, but it was okay. I was the luckiest girl alive. And I never wanted to forget it. "I love you too, Hal Amity. Merry Christmas."

"Merry Christmas, honey. And I'm hoping for many more just like it."

"Well," I said. "Maybe we could leave out the murder part."

He chuckled. "Maybe. But with you around, that seems increasingly improbable."

THE END

READ MORE COUNTRY COUSIN MYSTERIES

* * *

If you enjoyed **Rudolph the Red-Nosed Bumpkin**, you might want to check out the rest of the series. Please enjoy Chapter One of **Unlucky Bumpkin**, Book 5 of the *Country Cousin Mysteries* as my gift to you!

* * *

She's just a country girl who loves her dog...and her cat...and her pig. But protecting them from a killer might suck the sweet right out of her bucolic little world.

Pence Lucklin has always had the luck of the Irish, though he's about as far from Irish as you can get. It is, after all, how he got his nickname, Lucky

Lucklin. But it appears that his luck has run out in a big way. That's putting it mildly, I guess. Since Lucky just turned up dead, hanging from a tool hook at my family's auction business.

Was Lucky's death meant as a warning for me? Could this mean the return of an old villain? Will Hal and I be called on to help the local Deer Hollow police find a killer?

In the end, luck probably won't have much to do with the outcome. Luck can be made. And as death stalks the people I love, I'm fully prepared to force the hand of fate and create my own luck. Or die trying.

Grab your copy of Unlucky Bumpkin here: https://samcheever.com/books/#Country

UNLUCKY BUMPKIN

I stood in the gravel and stared past the high metal fence, topped with double rows of razor wire. The buildings in the distance were half shrouded in fog, their familiar lines softened in the mist. Somewhere along the side, lost in the thick mist, the squat stone ranch house that had served as an office waited for me to step through the door and begin the process of closing down what had once been an integral part of my life. Shutting a door I'd never be able to open again.

The sign attached to the wide gates proclaimed the hundred acre space to be *Fulle-Proof Auctions*. The auction had been my family's business for decades, until my parents had been believed killed in the crash of a private plane at the back of our property. I'd since learned I hadn't lost them both, but the past the acres of gravel and metal buildings represented had died along with my father in that small plane.

Beside me, Caphy whined softly, no doubt sensing my sadness. It had been a tough decision to sell the place. My dad had loved the auction. He'd built it from a tiny farm auction to a business that took in equipment of all sizes from around the country and brought top dollar for quality offerings.

Selling it now would be like severing the final link with my dad. To me if felt like cutting off a limb, leaving me bloodied, my memories set adrift in a mist not unlike the one surrounding Caphy and me in that moment.

But after much discussion, my mom and I had finally come to the only decision we could. The auction needed to be sold. My father wasn't coming back and neither my mom nor I would be running the business. Sitting empty, it was just a liability. Besides, I'd been recieving nearly daily calls from people who wondered when the auction would live again.

There were people who'd counted on the service my father once provided. It was time to let someone else provide it.

"It's okay, Caphy girl. I'm just feeling a little sad."

She swiped a wide wet tongue over my hand and gave her muscular tail a quick swipe over the ground. But her green gaze told me she wasn't buying it. She always had been able to read me like a book.

Headlights flashed through the mist and skimmed over us, followed by the soft rumble of a car engine. A big car.

Tears burned my eyes and I bit back a sob.

He'd come.

Somewhere down deep, I'd known he would. Though he had to have driven most of the night to get there in time.

The big SUV pulled up next to my car and stopped, the lights flaring into the dense mist as the Greek god behind the wheel extinguished the engine. The door opened and he was suddenly there, hurrying around the car to wrap me in arms that were strong and filled with comfort he'd known I'd need despite my assurances that I was fine.

"Hey," he said, his voice warm and rumbly against my ear as I pressed into him.

"Hey," I responded. "You came."

"Of course."

Hal had been on special assignment in Tennesee when I'd told him what I'd planned. He'd asked me to wait, but I knew I had to do it fast, like yanking off a bandaid, or I might not have had the will to do it at all. As it was I'd been awake most of the night, wavering back and forth about my decision. I'd nearly called Madge Watson, my realtor to cancel our appointment a few times.

For more than one reason, she wouldn't have thanked me. The biggest one being the fact that it had been the wee hours of the morning when I'd plucked my cell off the bedside table and fought with myself not to dial.

"Is the realtor here yet?" It was like he'd read my mind.

I shook my head. "She's not coming for a few hours. She needs to take pictures so she wants light. I wrinkled my nose. "And hopefully less fog."

He chuckled, one big hand rubbing my back in slow circles. "Did you bring boxes?"

"Some…"

He must have heard the struggle in my voice because he kissed the top of my head. "I brought some."

He knew me too well. Deep, deep down inside I was pretty sure I was indulging in a bit of self-sabotage. I'd brought far fewer boxes than I knew I'd need. Reluctant to take the final step of boxing up my dad's stuff.

I sighed, nodding.

"You have the key?"

I dug into the pocket of my jeans and handed it to him. "I'll see you inside." Suddenly unwilling to watch him unlock the gate, I hurried around my car and slid inside after Caphy. The strange resistance made me wonder how long I would have stood there if Hal hadn't shown up.

I was thinking it would have been a while.

Headlights cutting pale circles in the empty gravel between the gate and the office, I drove slowly into the complex and parked in front of the building. I forced myself to climb out of the car as Hal parked beside me. Caphy disappeared into the fog, tail happily wagging. She'd always loved the complex, no doubt finding it a delicious brew of scents and small skittering critters to harass.

Hal unlocked the door to the office as I stood staring off into the cloaking miasma, rubbing my arms. Sadness filled me at the sound of the door opening with a soft whoosh, stale air tumbling out to greet me. It was really going to happen.

I was going to sell Fulle-Proof Auctions.

I'd be severing a huge chunk of my memories and my childhood along with it.

And I was pretty sure I'd be slicing off a chunk of my heart too.

I carefully boxed up the things in the outer office first, intending to store them in the attic at home until my mom had a chance to go through them. As Hal carried the last box out of the building, I stood in the center of the space, memories of hours spent playing there as a child rolling over me.

The sights and sounds of those carefree days,

skewed by my childhood viewpoint and made more poignant through nostalgia, were like ghosts spinning through the room, long gone but never forgotten.

I'd sat in the dusty, threadbare armchair between the two office doors and played with my dolls, spinning tales of exciting adventures and happily ever afters until my mom yelled at me to go outside and play or, when I got a bit older, to do my homework.

The scarred wooden desk that dominated the outer office, which had once the living room of the small ranch house, had been my favorite place to spread my homework out when the office manager, Betty had gone home for the day. Thinking about the slightly overweight, middle-aged woman made me sad. I hadn't even known when she'd died a few weeks after my father's death. I'd been too deep into my own grief to notice. And I'd had no inkling until recently that the two deaths might have even been connected. Recalling the kind-hearted woman who'd always brought me treats, that made me immeasurably sad.

The door opened and Hal came in, the early morning sunshine behind him. "Madge is here."

I rubbed my dusty hands over my jeans and nodded, my gaze sliding toward the two closed office doors. As I headed outside to meet the realtor, I couldn't help feeling at least a little relieved to get a short reprieve from the task ahead of me.

Packing up my parents' offices.

We found Madge snapping pictures outside the biggest building. I was relieved to see that the bright sunshine had burned off the last of the fog, but its stark touch wasn't doing much to hide the fading and worn metal of the aging building.

Madge turned as I walked up, giving me a smile. "Mornin'."

I smiled back. "Hey, Madge. What do you think? Should I invest the money in getting these buildings painted?" I hated to do that. It would cost me a small fortune. But if it would help me get a better price for the auction, it might be worth doing.

"Let's hold off on that. I think I can maximize the potential with the right angles and lighting. And to tell you the truth, this auction is a goldmine. I don't think you'll have any trouble selling it."

Her words should have made me feel better. But a small part of me hoped it didn't sell for a while. I needed a few months to wrap my head around letting it go. "Shall we go inside?"

Hal and I started forward without waiting for her response and Madge fell into step beside us. Hal pulled the heavy doors of the main building open and we stepped through.

The past roared over me, nearly taking me to my knees. Hal grabbed my elbow as tears filled my eyes. I stared at the rows of bleachers down the long sides of the huge building, remembering how I'd played underneath them during the auctions, and clambered over them while my dad and Uncle Dev, my godfather and dad's lifelong best friend, had examined and discussed potential items for future auctions.

The sun formed perfect rectangles on the dusty ground, its light framed in clear sections of roof high above. The familiar smell, a mix of gasoline and sawdust, brought those days of adventure and endless possibilities back in a dizzying rush.

Hal bent his head to look me in the eyes. "Are you okay, honey?"

I sniffed, scraping the heel of my hand under my eyes. "I'm fine. It's just been a while since I've been in here."

"The building's in great shape," said Madge. She was twenty yards away, walking down the wide center aisle and assessing the property. "You won't have to do anything with this, Joey."

I nodded, relieved.

She stopped near the end and pointed at a small door. "What's that?"

"The annex," I called out to her, starting in her direction. "A mechanical room. Dad kept parts there in case something broke down on the day of an auction."

The "annex" was a second, smaller building built off the side of the main auction building and connected only by that small door. There was a larger, garage type door on the long side of the attached building so they could drive equipment into the annex for repairs. My father had always kept the annex locked securely up because the parts he kept inside tended to be worth a lot of money.

"You'll probably need to use the key," I told Hal as we joined Madge in front of the door.

Thank goodness my father'd had the foresight to key all the locks the same so only one key was needed for everything.

At the time, he'd said it was for expediency, but we'd both known it was because my mother always lost her keys. She could lose them walking from the front door to the car and never find them again.

It was a skill I luckily hadn't inherited.

Hal turned the key and the knob and shoved the door open.

We reared back in shock and revulsion.

"Ugh!" said Madge. "What is that?"

A foul stench I recognized all too well wafted out, sending us all stumbling back away from the door.

Death.

Check out the entire series here: https://samcheever.com/books/#Country

If you enjoyed **Rudolph the Red-Nosed Reindeer**, you might also enjoy these other fun mystery series by Sam. To find out more, visit the **BOOKS** page at www.samcheever.com:

Country Cousin Mysteries (More fun with Joey and Caphy!)
Gainfully Employed Mysteries
Honeybun Heat Series
Silver Hills Cozy Mysteries
Yesterday's Paranormal Mysteries
Reluctant Familiar Paranormal Mysteries
Enchanting Inquiries Paranormal Mysteries

ABOUT THE AUTHOR

Multiple-time USA Today and Wall Street Journal Best-selling Author Sam Cheever writes mystery and suspense, creating stories that draw you in and keep you eagerly turning pages. Known for writing great characters, snappy dialogue, and unique and exhilarating stories, Sam is the award-winning author of 80+ books.

To learn more about Sam and her work, visit her at one of her online hotspots:
www.samcheever.com
samcheever@samcheever.com